CHANCE TO DANCE FOR YOU

Gail Sidonie Sobat

GREAT PLAINS
TEEN FICTION

Great Plains Teen Fiction
(an imprint of Great Plains Publications)
345-955 Portage Avenue
Winnipeg, MB R3G 0P9
www.greatplains.mb.ca

Great Plains Publications gratefully acknowledges the financial support
provided for its publishing program by the Government of Canada
through the Book Publishing Industry Development Program (BPIDP);
the Canada Council for the Arts; the Province of Manitoba through the
Book Publishing Tax Credit and the Book Publisher Marketing Assistance
Program; and the Manitoba Arts Council.

All characters appearing in this work are fictitious. Any resemblance
to real persons, living or dead, is purely coincidental.

Design & Typography by Relish Design Studio Inc.

Printed in Canada by Friesens

Library and Archives Canada Cataloguing in Publication

Sobat, Gail Sidonie,
    Chance to dance for you / Gail Sidonie Sobat.

ISBN 978-1-926531-11-3
I. Title.

PS8587.O23C43 2011   jC813'.6   C2010-907647-8

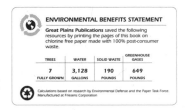

For Mark Andrew Haroun
Disco Dance Partner
Beloved Friend
Goat Slayer

ONE

On the Street Where You Live

I live where you live.

There are pretty tree-lined streets. The asphalt is even and unpockmarked, unlike my adolescent skin which is currently sprouting a massive zit, not to mention my other scars…the ones you can't see. The ones that come of living the cliché of a tortured adolescence.

A little river, a brook really, bisects the town-cum-city. The houses are ordered into architecturally-controlled districts. Some have only cedar-shingled roofs. Some are gated communities. None of the colours is offensive to the eye or brighter than beige.

Every house has a fence.

The streets are named, not numbered, which makes it difficult to get around this pretty, pretty place.

We live in the bird section. Birdwood. I'd like to say we live on Cuckoo Street, but that would be lying. There's no such street. We reside at 22 Oriole Crescent. In a modest house, unlike our neighbours to the north and east. Who live in wannabe mansions. A zillion windows. Interior designer furniture. Two furnaces each to heat their humungous homes. And of course, their three-car garages.

Not that I'm jealous or anything.

I go to one of three high schools in this boring borough. W. E. Whitleigh. Named after a dead white guy.

Oh, I should mention that our affluent suburb is mostly made up of white people. Despite the Métis who first settled here. After the Cree, of course, who first lived near the little river in our valley for who knows how many hundreds of years. But no one cares about that now. This community has been nicely sanitized of all that messiness. Well, almost. And most of its colour.

And in the little town-city that wishes it were a big city are all the shops and restaurants you'd find anywhere else in North America. A tidy strip runs straight through Turid Park, dividing it east and west. And on the tidy strip is the Canadian Tire, the A&W, the mighty golden arches, the Mr. Lube, the Shell and Esso and Petrocan, all vying for your dollar to fill up any one of your two cars and one SUV so we can all go merrily along raising the global temperature.

I'm in the environmental/human rights club at school. It's about the only thing I do at school. Besides dance, that is.

Despite its glossy surface, there's a dark underside to this small-town city, as if you didn't already know that. A shadow cast by the nice white folks who live here. This place, like yours, has lots of secrets.

For instance, Mrs. Theodore, my Spanish teacher, is married to a nice man who sells cars for a living. He owns the dealership. I like Spanish. But not the way she teaches it. Her nice husband is having quite an affair with one of his much younger employees. We all know her. She graduated from Whitleigh three summers ago. Mrs. Theodore holds up her head and goes on conjugating irregular verbs. I guess that's the sacrifice you make for the three-car garage, the nice neighbourhood and every kitchen appliance you could ever wish for.

My drama teacher, and I do like her, is also having an affair. With a brown man. I think Mrs. Theodore caught them coming out of the darkened drama room one night after school. Nowadays Ms. Sbuda doesn't look very happy. When she smiles her eyes don't get involved. She's still a very good teacher—I love drama—but she's somewhere else. Guess that's what happens when you're up to shenanigans with a brown man in a white school after hours.

I have it on good authority that the handsome music teacher, Mr. Ritz, was in rehab over the summer. Good thing, too. I ran into him after dance rehearsal last spring reeking of weed. Him not me. Then rumours were flying that he had a cold. One of those that never end. The kind where you're always sniffling. Then he was missing a lot of school. And then one day he was just gone. The final band concert was cancelled. But he's back now. I guess over the summer he also found his lord and saviour. He runs the Christian reading club. I hear that before every band concert there's a group prayer. Good thing there are no Muslims or Jews or Buddhists in the band, or in our school for that matter.

And I guess that over the summer Miss Dayton lost her baby. Poor thing. Apparently, she'll be rejoining us in term two. Until then she's on stress leave. I guess she has until January 7th to patch her life back together. Good to know that she found out about Paxil.

I also know for a fact, and so do you if you read the papers, that Mrs. Wilson's husband embezzled money from the securities company he works for. Used to work for. I rode my bike past their beautiful house, now empty and for sale. She's living with her sister, these days. He's gone to jail. Saw the news photo of him in a prison-issue jumpsuit. Sadly though, orange was never his colour. Mrs. Wilson teaches physics. Not my favourite class, though I'm good at physics, and it's the one I share with Jess Campeau.

Jess Campeau, the most gorgeous and popular guy in the school. On the football team. The town hockey star.

Jess Campeau, the pig. Who smears me and my friends—especially my best friend, Tilly—with his filthy mouth every chance he gets.

Jess Campeau.

But I digress.

Did I mention that my principal, okay, ex-principal, the ineffectual and almost invisible Mr. Dibson, is gay? He left principalship for real estate and fell madly in love with a fellow broker. Then he left his wife. And kids. And heterosexuality far behind. Somebody spray-painted *Mr. Dibson is a fudge-packer* all over the back bricks of the school. I have a strong hunch who did it. Now we have a new principal, Mr. Kato, who drags his fat ass around the hallways picking out his favourites and picking on the misfits. Guess which category I fall into? I miss Mr. Dibson.

Which brings me to my point. In a nice white suburb, in a nice white neighbourhood, in a nice white school, I just don't fit. I am incongruent. I guess such places are good for guys who are hockey players (not mentioning any names) or girls like Tilly who love soccer. But where does a kid like me fit in?

Kids like me are prey. Especially for kids like Jess Campeau. For example.

I was in the gym locker room. Changing. Did I mention that I loathe and detest the gym change room? It's been the site of much derision and humiliation. So I loitered in the can, waiting until everyone else had changed and left the room. Then I went to my locker and was fiddling nervously with the lock. Guess who sneaked up behind me? He should have been long gone to his next class by then. He was definitely violating my boundaries. Not that he cared or even knew about those.

Jess Campeau spun me around. Pressed me into the lockers with his ripped torso. I could hardly breathe. And then he kissed me on the mouth. I mean really kissed me. Deeply. And I confess that I melted and kissed him back. Then he hissed in my ear.

"If you tell anyone, ANYONE, I will rip off your balls and stuff them in your mouth!"

How romantic.

Then I watched as the love and the enemy of my life straightened up and strutted out of the guys' change room.

TWO

Don We Now Our Gay Apparel

Yes, it's true. I am a fudge-packer, too. A queer. A homo. A fag. A flaming faggot. All nice expressions I've heard come out of Jess Campeau's mouth.

I'm the only guy in the dance class. I am a total loser at any kind of organized team sport. But shit, can I dance.

As the only boy in the dance class of the dance studio attached to our school, I am easily victimized. Ostracized. I am so visible, I might as well be the poster boy for gaydom.

I'd like to be a real boy. Like Pinocchio. Except that when I think of other real boys I'd like to emulate, it's not my nose that grows.

I'm a secret. And I'm not. They'd like to deny I exist. But of course, I do.

I've never confessed that I'm gay. Except to Tilly. Okay. And my mom, but it wasn't really a confession. I try to play straight, and Tilly plays that she's my girlfriend. I don't have limp wrists or any such faggotty attributes. I dress like other guys. And I avoid other guys. Especially…

But, of course, they found me out. Especially when the biggest homophobe of all was directing his ugliness daily at me. Until that moment in the dressing room, I thought I was the only queer in the school of eight hundred students, even though the odds suggested there had to be others.

I just didn't think it could be Jess Campeau.

What the hell!

I hovered between hot and scared. What to do with this new secret knowledge? And exactly what were the rules here?

Well, I tried to find out after the football practice that Tuesday night. I flew out of dance class and over to the playing field as the football game was wrapping up. Whitleigh won. What else is new? We were in the semi-finals. And our star was being hoisted above the heads of the team players. I watched it all in a daze, from the sideline shadows, thinking this guy, this football jock hero, Jess Campeau, kissed me, Ian Trudeau. Like he meant it. At least I thought he did.

I hung around the bleachers as the teams dispersed to the dressing rooms. Damn near froze my ass off waiting for him. It was October dark, but when he came out I knew which way he was headed. Across the field and through the little wood. I knew where he lived. I've followed him home before. Yes, I know I sound like a pathetic stalker, but like I said, I both hated and was attracted to this guy. For a long time, too. At least since the beginning of my first year of high school.

We were in the spindly copse of trees. Okay, they're spindly but sufficient. He dropped his pack and turned on me. "What the hell are you doing?"

"I…I…" And then and there my smart mouth failed me. Utterly.

"Christ, Trudeau. What are you thinking?" Jess took a step closer. I was terrified he might hit me. But he really only hit on the field. And with his homophobic comments.

"I c-couldn't believe wh-what happened. L-last week. I mean."

Another step closer. He dropped his equipment bag. "Nothing happened! Nothing." And then he grabbed me and pushed me again, this time up against a tree. And he did it like before. Kissed me. And I kissed him back. And my heart was pounding so I thought

I would puke. Something crazy happened to my breathing. And to those little tiny, gossamer hairs along my neck. And then he pulled away. And I could tell it took him some effort to do it, too.

"So I wasn't dreaming."

"Shut up, will you?" Jess's voice was filled with self-revulsion. I know what that's all about. All I wanted was to reach out to him. To help him.

But he shoved me aside. Grabbed his stuff and took off. "Don't follow me home again," he spat. Then he left me there. Shivering, I watched him trudge away.

So it appeared that Jess Campeau got to make the rules. He got to come on to me and just decide he was going to kiss me whenever. And I was just to be ready for it. In the meantime, I was supposed to shut up and take his stupid comments like always and pretend that Jess Campeau wasn't as much a flaming homo as I am!!

I texted Tilly: *Jess Campeau wants me.*

LMAO.

He stuck his tongue down my throat.

Say what?

Snogged me in the change room.

!!!

I know!

Where r u?

Almost at home.

I am so coming over right now!

I could hear that screechy excited voice she gets right through her text message.

So I told her. Everything.

"Shut up!"

"It's all true. I'm not making any of it up."

"Is he any good?"

"Well, considering he is the first and only guy I have ever deep-kissed, and the only person—period—I've kissed besides my parents and you and that one guy at summer camp, I'd say yeah, he's pretty good." Tilly and I once had a brief attempt at a romance. It was quickly aborted when neither of us really felt much of anything. Except friendship. She is a great friend.

"Sweet. But he's such an asshole."

As if on cue, Jann Arden's "Insensitive" came on the stereo. "Perfect!" we said in unison. We're like that. A good team. We can read each other. And we often like the same guys. Which makes for great conversation.

"It's obviously a cover-up. His homophobia. A ruse to deflect attention."

Tilly smacked her gum and nodded at me. "Yeah, but he can't keep doing this to you. Either he's in or he's out. Can't be both. It's not fair to you."

"Or healthy for him."

"So what."

"So what? It's got to be tough, is what. How the hell does the jock of the school, of the burb, who has every girl following him…"

"Not every girl! Not this girl, for example!"

"Ok, almost every girl (and one particular guy) following him and wanting him, deal with the fact that everyone THINKS he's this great macho straight man when in fact he's queer as folk."

"Hey, has the DVD of the final season of that arrived at Movie Studio?"

"Not until the end of the month."

"Maybe we can just download it…"

"Will you answer me please, Tilly?"

"Well, I don't feel particularly sorry for him. Look what he says to people. Girls. You. How he struts around like King bloody Tut with everyone—teachers, administrators, groupies—fawning all over him like his shit don't stink. I'm glad he's got this secret. That he's obviously screwed up about it. Good. Mr. Popularity's popularity hangs by a thread. And you, Ian," she pointed her finger at me, "hold the scissors. I'm sure that makes him very, very nervous."

I thought about that. I could really make Jess's life uncomfortable. Miserable even. It's kind of a rush, that power. And it's true. Jess has said unkind things to so many girls. Comments on their weight. Their hair. Rating their faces. Their bodies. In that way, he's not unlike the other bozos who haunt the halls of suburban schools, I guess. I tried to persuade Tilly. "But then that's part of it, isn't it? He wants to be seen and perceived as just any other guy. Don't we all wish we could be normal? Fit in?"

"Do we?" Tilly turned our faces to the mirror on my bedroom wall. "Look at us. Do we want to be normal? Whatever that is."

It's okay to be different around Tilly. To be pretty smart. To be a dancer. To be gay. I looked at her reflection looking at me. "I've wished for most of my juvenile life to be like the other guys. To be straight, Tilly."

"What a shame."

"Yeah, it is. But this is the world we live in, isn't it? Look at what happens to nice gay boys. They get bullied. Bashed. Bloodied. Or worse. Remember Tyler Clementi. Matthew Shepard."

"I know." After all, she is in the human rights/environmental club, SPAM (Students Promoting Active Movement), with me. So we know about recent statistics on gay teen suicide. And about Matthew Shepard. How just over ten years ago he was taken. Tortured. Tied to a Wyoming fence like a scarecrow. Left to die. And he did. Tracks of tears down his blood-soaked face.

"It hurts to be gay, Tilly."

She put her arms around me. "I know, Ian, I know."

THREE
Meet Me Halfway

I resolved to just watch Jess Campeau for a few days. See what his next move, if any, might be.

I trailed him and tried to keep my distance at the same time. Averted my gaze whenever I happened upon him. Never looked once at him in physics. He ignored me, but I still felt his eyes on me occasionally. I avoided the gym and the football practice field. I kept this up for three days. And Tilly spied on him, too. We took notes. When I'd amassed enough evidence, I worked up the nerve to phone him one evening at home. I'd long ago looked up and memorized his phone number. As if, I told myself. As if you'll ever actually call him. And suddenly here I was.

Now my finger actually trembled as I pushed the buttons.

A female voice answered.

"Hello, can I talk to Jess?"

I heard his mother calling him in the distance.

"Hullo." What a great voice he has, I thought.

"Hi Jess. It's me. Ian." I held my breath, hoping he wouldn't hang up on me.

"What the hell are you doing?" he hissed.

"Are you somewhere private where you can talk to me?"

"No!"

"Can you move to another phone?"

"NO!"

"Jess," I tried to control the tremolo in my voice, "look, we need to talk. It's either this or I confront you in the hallway."

The phone was silent. "Fine. Hold on."

I heard him asking his mother to hang up the extension. Then the click of his pick-up in another room and the second click of the first phone. "What do you want, Trudeau?"

"I could ask you the same thing, Jess."

"I don't want anything from you."

"Except my vow of silence."

"Ex-except that, yeah."

"Ok. Then we need to work an exchange."

"What?"

"We need a deal, Jess."

He paused. "What kind of deal?"

I took a deep breath. "If you want my vow of silence, then you have to make some changes."

"What?"

"In the past three days, you have uttered seventeen slurs against females—"

"What?"

"—and made exactly eight homophobic comments—"

"Screw you!"

"—within earshot of me and my peers."

"You're a friggin' weirdo, you know that Trudeau!"

"It has to stop, Jess. It has to. Or I will make it known to the student body, the teaching staff, the entire football team and coaching staff—"

"You are so dead, Trudeau…"

"—and your parents," I heard him swallow, "that you, Jess Campeau, are a fag."

There was another silence, a long silence.

"It's not an unfair request, Jess. You're hurting people with your slanderous remarks. You're hurting girls. You're hurting me."

"So what?"

"And most important, you're hurting yourself."

I let that sink in, then continued. "I'm not being unreasonable. I just want the misogyny and the homophobia to stop."

"The what?"

"Stop slagging the girls and the homos, Jess! Do that, and I'll keep my mouth shut."

"Maybe…"

"And Jess?"

"I'm listening."

"One more thing. I'll be your friend."

He snorted.

"I mean it, Jess. I'll be a good friend. And you need a friend like me."

"I don't need your friendship, Trudeau."

"Yes, you do."

"What the hell do I need you for?"

I swallowed the little frog that threatened my voice. "Well, you already know why from your own actions. But more than that you need someone who gets it, Jess."

"I need a little faggot dancer boy, exactly why?"

"Jess!"

"Sorry. I–I'm sorry."

He paused. I waited.

"I already got lots of friends."

"Do you? Do you really? Then why do I have to keep everything such a secret if you've got so many good buddies?"

From the other side of our special little burb, Jess Campeau sighed deeply. "Ok. I'll tone down the language. Shut my big mouth. But…"

"But what?"

"We can't be friends, Ian."

"We already are, Jess. You crossed a line. You can't go back. Now I'm offering you a chance to be around someone who knows who you are, what you are. Even if it is our little secret."

FOUR

WTF?

You might well ask what I was doing in the guys' change room that fateful day when Jess Campeau kissed me. If you're a 'mophobe like so many of the fine denizens of our little plastic suburban bubble, you might think I was cruising. Like all fags do. We predators on the prowl for straight young men in their prime.

Rest assured: that's just another urban myth we can lay to rest.

So wtf *was* a nice gay boy like me doing in a place like the über-macho gymnasium dressing room?

In fact, I was there on legitimate football business. Yes, indeed. I was solicited by Coach Magee for the purposes of dexterity and finesse movement training with the famed Whitleigh Wailers. And a more apt name for a football team has never been chosen. They are a bunch of wailers. Not to mention graceless goons. Sure, they've got punch and brawn. But Coach Magee, fresh out of university where he coached his team to the championships, has some far-fetched and rattle-brained ideas about turning these brutish rams into sure-footed bucks.

Get this: dance training makes for better agility, higher leaps, fewer injuries among football players.

Who knew?

Well apparently, defensive back Donovin Darius did. So too, Pittsburgh Steelers' wide receiver, Lynn Swann. And UK

Manchester United's Rio Ferdinand, star of that other kind of football known as soccer, once won a ballet scholarship and yearned to be a dancer!

It's true! I have it on excellent authority! Tilly Monpetit! And she knows practically everything there is to know about soccer.

Coach Magee had heard about me and Leonora Pinkoski—aka prima ballerina principessa—doing agility and strength training with the cross-country ski team last winter. Of course, they're an all-girl team and cross-country hasn't nearly the sport sex appeal or the straight-male we-can't-be-seen-with-or-as-homos associations. But the team won provincials and the x-country coach, Ms. Moyer, gave us a lot of credit. She even bought us gift certificates to Tim Hortons. Which was nice. I love a good French cruller.

So when Magee asked me to work with his football boys, colour me crazy, but this rainbow boy agreed.

My first day was like walking into the dragon's den. The coach introduced me. Silence and sullen stares. A few of them spit, as football brutes do. I could see they hated being there. Hated me. For putting them in this humiliating position. You know the one. They always assume.

But Magee was onto the negative vibe and told the guys that there would be no snide remarks on or off field, in or out of the gym. Which is where we practise. Behind closed doors. Otherwise, they'd never live it down. Working with me, that is.

I'm sure they thought that we'd be doing limp-wristed, arm-flapping, en pointe femme maneuvers galore.

But no. I got those broad-backed boys a-sweating. We crossed that gym floor. We travelled. We worked on jumping. Landing with precision. On height in our jumps. On foot dexterity. On aerobic stamina. On core strength. And on flexibility, which face it, many pigskin jocks just don't have.

Two months we'd been honing skills, twice each week. I'm not one to take credit where it's not due, but the team was on a winning streak. Tilly and I went to watch a few games. Incognito, bundled up in our toques and scarves and bulky down jackets. I'd get quite excited when Whitleigh scored, though I had no idea what the hell was going on most of the time. I just knew that when Jess Campeau had the ball, I'd yell my guts out. He was wonderful in a full-out run.

Tilly called him "buns of steel."

I didn't disagree.

Too bad he's such a jerkoff.

But I digress.

Coach Magee called me his wild card and insisted that I continue working with the team until semi-finals. I was coping pretty well. Hell, Tilly and I even had a great yuk-alicious moment when we watched our new fave TV show, *Glee*. Right there on the flat screen, we saw it. Art imitating life! The token homosexual boy character, Kurt, played by actor Chris Colfer, was teaching the football team dance moves. Of course, it was all overblown and choreographed, completely unrealistic and set to music. Nothing like real life. But way more fun! Tilly and I downloaded the song from the show that night from iTunes.

Like I said, I was coping.

Until the kiss at the scene of the crime.

I certainly had noticed and watched and coached Jess Campeau for two months. Admired him, as always, from afar. But I hadn't seen a flicker of his interest in me. And of course, out of the gym and away from Coach Magee, his boorish behaviour resumed. But maybe it lessened towards me directly. Or maybe I imagined that. One thing I guess I realized later is that he shut the guys up when I was talking or instructing during practice. Got their attention on my behalf. But that never added up to more than him taking his usual leadership stance.

But then what could he do to show interest in someone like me? There's no such thing as a gay jock, star athlete. Or so the world would like to believe. He had to stay under the radar. And my gaydar was clearly malfunctioning.

So that kiss bitch-slapped me.

I always wanted to be in a relationship. To be in love. And all the stuff that goes with it. Hell, I'm an all-Canadian boy. Who just happens to play for the other team. When I learned that Jess also plays for my team, my heart went a little ballistic. And I guess I joined the ranks of those I formerly used to pity: the love-sick with their oft-repeated refrains. The stuff of bad love songs.

Could I have him? Couldn't I? How could I, given where we live, the school we attend? Why couldn't I? After all, this *is* the twenty-first century. But then again, fag-bashers are still with us. Thriving, in many cases and places. Like the one where I live. There was an incident in the paper that same week about a young man jumped because he was a suspected homosexual by his attackers. In our very own loving borough.

So what if we defied the odds? Did Jess want to? Did he want me? Did he have the guts to come out? I doubted it.

And why should he? He has everything going for him. He is celebrated. Adored. Sought after by the masses. He is popular.

I'm not.

Except that he is gay. So am I.

I could…maybe be his friend. I could maybe be *his*.

If he wanted to. If he wanted me.

Shit.

Life had suddenly become very complicated.

Love or infatuation or whatever this was, made it hard to concentrate. On work. On school. On training. On anything but Jess Campeau.

I felt like a stupid fourteen-year-old love-sick girl. Kind of like Leonora Pinkoski who is always in love with some new guy every other week. She drives me to distraction with her broken-hearted laments. The girl is a flake. Even if she is a superb dancer and my arch-competitor.

The night I phoned Jess, I realized I'd sat through an entire afternoon of social and math classes writing nothing down except Jess Campeau's name.

OMG! I was turning into a flakey, love-smitten, obsessively idiotic ballerina.

Gag me. Please. Somebody.

FIVE
Won't You Take Me To Funk E-Town?

We met privately for the first time in the Big City. The one to which our suburb and the other Xerox copies are attached like spokes of a wheel. The Big City is safe. The Big City has coffee shops where young gay males can meet and talk in anonymity, then go home and pretend like they don't even know each other.

It took me three buses and two hours to get to the trendy arts district where we met. It took Jess about twenty-five minutes. He has a car.

As it was I got there first. I watched his entrance to the café. Cool. Unhurried. Sure of himself. He looked like one of those excellent Calvin Klein models that we all drool over. You know. Hair slightly messy. Day-old stubble. Hands in tight jean pockets. Trendy down jacket. Nonchalant as all hell.

I watched him looking for me. Tried to keep my heart from leaping across the room at him. I waved.

And Jess Campeau sauntered over to me. Sat down at my table. Where I sat, heated up as my pumpkin spiced latté.

"Want a coffee? My treat."

"Do they have any thing like… Gatorade?"

He really was a walking stereotype. Except that, of course, he wasn't. "I'll go see."

I got up and went to the counter. No Gatorade, so I got him some kind of high-energy fruit juice smoothie thing. I could feel his eyes on me. I was glad I'd gone with Tilly's suggestion of the navy zip sweater.

I turned around, drink in hand, and tried to stride confidently, smilingly back to the table. I don't think he saw my hand shake as I set down the smoothie. He seemed to be looking anywhere else. Especially not at me or my face.

We turned our attention to our drinks. He gulped. I sipped. Then I sighed.

"Look, Jess. I know this is awkward for you. It's awkward for me, too. But we've got to start somewhere. We can't keep having… you know… encounters in the locker room."

He looked at me then.

"You must be having a hard time of it. I mean… you're the high school star. All kinds of expectations are on you. You're popular. No wonder you've had to hide who you are, Jess. You're your own dirty little secret."

"Yup."

"Except that you're not. You're not dirty. And you won't always have to be a secret."

He just listened to me. Looked at me. Drank his smoothie.

I used my best it's-ok-to-be-gay voice. "You're not an aberration, a freak of nature, Jess."

"My dad says so."

My eyebrows shot up. "He knows???"

"No, stupid. He'll never know. It's just what he thinks of homos. They're… we're all freaks and child molesters. You should hear him, man." Pain came into Jess's voice. "He's got nothin' good to say about any queer or dyke. Feels they should be aborted in the womb. Or put off on some island to homo around together away from the rest of the normal people."

"Jeez. I'm sorry, Jess."

"My old man would hate me. I can't ever let him know."

"Well, one day you'll have to, Jess. Or leave home for good. Or live in the closet and be miserable trying to be someone you're not for the rest of your life."

"I hate talking about this."

"Ok. What would you rather talk about?"

"I dunno."

I took a shot. "Does your mom know? Your siblings?"

"No. My mom keeps pretty quiet. Dad definitely wears the pants, you know. I haven't got a brother or a sister. I'm an only child."

"Me, too."

"So I'm the major disappointment. The only one."

"Why's that?"

"Because I don't want to go into the army. My dad's in the Forces. I've been an army brat moving around my whole life."

"Where all have you lived?"

"Cold Lake. Petawawa, Ontario. Chilliwack, BC. Gagetown, New Brunswick. Now here."

"Wow. You've moved so many times."

"So far, it's been the best thing because I could just fade away before anyone could find out. I don't have any connections with the places we've lived."

"But now?"

"Now here. In just a couple of years, I sort of became an instant..."

"Celebrity."

"Yeah that."

"Must be hard, Jess."

He locked his eyes with mine. I swallowed my desire. Tried to concentrate on being his friend.

"It is."

"Then isn't it a relief that someone you can trust knows the truth?"

"Kind of."

"You picked me," I realized suddenly, "because you knew. Somehow you knew you could trust me."

Jess nodded. "I guess. That and..." He grinned.

And I blushed. Jess Campeau was attracted to me. Physically. That was nice to know. Incredibly flattering. But it also made me feel great that there was something more. Something about me that was recognizably trustworthy. Something of integrity that Mr. Monaghan, our social teacher, is always going on about.

We both looked around the room.

I made another offer. "I'm sorry about your dad. Anytime you want to talk about him, Jess, about anything, you should call me."

Jess shrugged. "I might."

"Maybe one day you can tell him..."

"He'll kill me. I know it."

I didn't know what to say to that. I honestly didn't. Jess was so vehement. He really believed his own words. I can't imagine a father wanting to kill his own son. But then I can't really imagine having a father. Mine took off shortly after I was born. Well, "took off" is a relative term. His taking off was sort of helped along by a restraining order and some good lawyers paid for by my grandparents. Since then I've never even seen the whites of his eyes, except in pictures. It's a good thing, too. He was abusive to my mom. So I've never met him, and I don't want to. He abandoned us and hurt her. Who wants to know a father like that? But I know other kids' fathers. For instance, Tilly's dad is pretty cool, even if his jokes are lame. But Jess's dad sounded ugly. Violent.

"Has he ever hurt you?"

Jess looked steadily at the football ring on his right hand.
"Has he?"

"Let's just say he has a temper. A bad temper."

"Shit, Jess."

He slurped the last of his drink up through the straw. Then stood abruptly. "Let's go somewhere."

"Where?"

"I dunno. For a walk."

"Ok." I pulled on my fleece and down vest. Wondered if I should put up my hoodie. Vanity prevailed. I opted to freeze my ears off rather than look like a geek beside Jess.

We walked out of the café and into the cold late afternoon light. He was so silent. I really wanted to hold his hand. But that would never do. So I shoved my hands in my pockets.

Several blocks later, he turned north towards the river. I trudged along, trying not to slip on the icy sidewalks. Trying not to be afraid of what would happen if I did fall and hurt myself. If Madame, my slightly mad dance coach, saw me then, she would have had a hairy fit.

We stopped at a park bench overlooking the river valley. The lights were just beginning to twinkle on in the city buildings above the north shore. There was one of those slivers of moon that sometimes come up on an early winter's evening. I was feeling awash in romantic thoughts. Despite the fact my ass was freezing.

Jess sniffed. He must have been cold, too, because he stood up suddenly. "I saw you, you know?"

"Huh?" I rose beside him.

"Dancing. The first time I ever saw you, in fact. That dance thing last fall."

"I remember. I saw you, too. I saw you look at me. But I had no idea that you were... you know... looking at me. That way. You know."

It had been a fall fundraiser. A dance review for cancer, put together by my teacher Madame Branislov. I'd danced with Leonora from the ballet school. Leonora the fourteen-year-old dance diva. Destined for stardom, or so she thinks. I thought Jess had been admiring her.

He turned to me, put his hands on my shoulders. Jess stood about four inches taller.

"Looking at you?" He smiled and I felt the corners of the world go all wonky. "I couldn't take my eyes off you."

And then we were doing exactly what I'd been wishing for secretly all afternoon. What had burbled away hopefully in my stomach since I'd invited him out. And suddenly it wasn't so chilly anymore.

When we looked up from each other, the sun had definitely set.

"You're shivering." He straightened my down vest.

"A l-little," I chattered.

"C'mon. I'll drive you home."

Gradually, I thawed out on the drive back to our rotten little burb. His tunes were great. Ben Harper.

"I like your taste. In music. And in cars..." I admired the Mustang. He'd worked on it with his father. It was vintage '70s he told me. Bright red with black vinyl interior.

His face in profile was perfect. "And I like your taste in men."

He grinned over at me. I thought I would pass out. From happiness. And other stuff I was feeling.

One good thing about Oriole Crescent is that a streetlamp down the way is perpetually burned out. Like I said, we live in the barely middle class neighbourhood of an otherwise rich-ass satellite community. City workers aren't nearly so fussy about appearances—or streetlights—out our way. Usually, that's annoying. This night it was perfect.

I pulled away from him.

He mumbled, "Wanna see a movie sometime?"

Duh. "Sure."

"Ok. I'll text you or something."

"O-ok." In disbelief, I slammed his car door. Watched him drive away. Wow. A red Mustang.

Then I tore off home. Tore into my room. Facebooked Tilly and told her everything.

Naturally.

Status: Ian Trudeau is over the sliver of a moon!

SIX

Dancing Queen

I've always danced.

My mom says I came dancing out of the womb. That I danced in that bouncy baby thing *les enfants* all get tucked into at some time or other.

I danced while my mother taught piano lessons. Endless piano lessons. Endless dancing.

I remember dancing for Gramma and Grampa when I was only a drooling tot. And I remember my first dance class.

I was six.

And I became instantly passionate about two things. Leaping and leotards.

God. I was a little fag. But cute. My mom has the picture of me in my first dance recital on the piano. I am Autumn. Dressed in red and gold leaves. I danced with the other figures of fall: acorns, oak leaves, pumpkin, but I got the leading role. Meaning I got to sprinkle leaves around the stage and prance around the others, making fall happen.

I was in my glory, little show-off that I was. Am.

I still want the lead. Not much has changed.

And I guess in the case of Jess Campeau, that's still kind of true.

I've been studying dance seriously since I was eight.

My mother, the piano teacher, works very hard to make ends meet and to send me to dance classes. Luckily, my grandparents help her and me out by subsidizing my lessons. Luckily, one of the best dance instructors in the greater urban area lives within the confines of our burrowing borough: Madame Isadora Branislov. Luckily, she defected from the USSR twenty years ago and came to Canada. Where she settled in Toronto and ran some hoity-toity hot-ass dance studio and choreographed dances on occasion with the National Ballet School for years... until some disgrace. Which she won't talk about and I'm dying to discover.

Personally, I think it was a bad ending to some love affair with a director or principal dancer.

Or else that she hit the bottle quite hard.

But maybe that just came after the disgrace.

Anyway, lucky for me that she's here now. Although she's a fading flower, she's a distinguished teacher. Hard-nose to the grindstone. A formidable task-mistress. Frankly, sometimes she's a bitch. But we all love Madame. Or at the very least, admire her. And fear her.

And I am her star. Her great hope.

Ok. Me and Leonora Pinkowski. We're Madame's prizes, as she likes to call us in her thick, smoke-tinged accent.

"Ee-an." That's how she pronounces my name. "Ee-an, my prize."

"Yes, Madame."

"Keep practising and building strong, young muscles. You will be king of leap! Da?"

"Da, Madame."

"Ee-an." We were outside the dance studio and she was lighting up a cigarette. One of those long, elegant numbers. "Don't ever to start smoking, do you hear Madame?"

"Yes, Madame."

"Gooood boy. You will grow to be Baryshnikov, da?" She exhaled smoke in my face.

"I hope so, Madame."

"There is no hopink, Ee-an. There is only to doing. If you don't belief, you will not. Do you understand?"

"Yes, Madame."

"Do you belief?"

"Yes, Madame."

"Gooood, my prize."

And I do belief. Believe. It is the one thing I most believe in the world. That I am a dancer. A damn fine dancer. Destined for greatness. Because Madame beliefs in me. Not to mention my mom, Gramma and Grampa, and, of course, Tilly. I've got a team of believers covering my back. And because of all that, I believe.

I'm really very lucky.

Except that I'm a gay boy, living in a very conservative, tight-ass community. Where the fundamentalists get together every Sunday in thirteen various but related churches to preach what an abomination I am, and others like me are.

A group of the mothers in a certain faction of this religious community even fought the school board and tried to get the dance school attached to Whitleigh High closed down because, as we all know, dancing leads to sex. Thank god the school board shooed them away. The school board knows that its bread is buttered by our dance school. We're a cash cow for them. Many little girls and girl-tweens and teens dance, meaning their well-heeled parents pay, meaning the school board can charge a nice high rent and get its reputation boosted as an arts supporter, to boot. Many photo opportunities. Good optics. Everybody's happy. Except for that group of mothers. They took their children out of Whitleigh over to the Catholic school. I guess the Catholics are lesser devils than the dancers.

And then there are my school fellows, many of whom I avoid. Who am I kidding? I avoid most of them. Except the guys in my drama class. They're okay. One of them even got pushed around behind the school. Robert Irons. Just because he's in drama. And a bit of a dweeb. Drama + dweeb = fag. So some macho-men decided that they would pick on Robert, a slip of a grade-ten boy. Not much happened to the attackers. A three-day suspension. Now Robert never goes out back of the school. Even though that's the direct route home for him. He circles all the way round the front and up the block and then heads home. He knows better. It's one of those things you learn about Whitleigh. There are no-go zones.

If you're not a smoker, you don't cross the street to be with the smoker gang. They're a mixture of girls trying to keep their weight down, guys from automotives, and heavy metal lovers who can be okay or assholes, depending on the day of the week or the direction of the wind.

If you're not an athlete, stay away from the gym at all costs during lunch hour and after school. You're plain not welcome, unless you're someone's friend or girlfriend, or just an adoring jock groupie, meaning you have to be straight.

If you're not a skater, if you don't like the music, don't know the lingo, don't go out to the paved courtyard—you are permanently uninvited.

And most important, if you're not a druggie or if you're in any way different or unpopular, don't go out back. That's where the student parking lot is. That's where trouble is for kids like me. It's no-faggots land.

So where do misfit kids like Robert and me go? Well, there's the library. It's a neutral zone. And the librarian, Mrs. Nesbitt, gets it. She gets that kids like me need a safe zone. So I hang out there once or twice a week. I see Robert in there, too. And Mrs. Nesbitt finds books for me. Stuff for my classes, if I need. And books on dance. I read the new biography on Nureyev that she ordered, I think especially for me. There's the music room for the music kids. The drama room, where the serious drama types hang out. Certain kids mill about the foods studies room, looking for free meals. And I know a girl who used to eat her lunch in a bathroom stall to avoid being seen or worse.

Her name is Tilly.

But things have been better for her this year and last since Ms. McDonald, the soccer coach, came to school. Tilly's always played soccer, since she was a little kid. But there was no school soccer program until two years ago at Whitleigh High. Until then, she was a lost girl milling about the halls, avoiding eyes, avoiding notice. Feeling completely useless and unnecessary.

No wonder she picked me for a friend. We have a lot in common. And we met in junior high, just when I began to sprout acne pimples and her dad got laid off from his pipeline job. For the first time. It's happened again since. Both the pimples and the layoffs. But I've discovered Exposed for acne, or my mom did. And Mr. Monpetit keeps getting hired back by Syncrude. So all's well that ends well.

I helped Tilly pick up her books from the mud where the grade nine girls had thrown them one fine, almost-but-not-quite spring day. I gave her my windbreaker to wrap around her pants dripping with slush because the fearsome femmes had also pushed Tilly in the mud and snowbank. All this at the bus stop where these lovely rituals sometimes play out between the affluent and poor groups of our suburb. Guess which one Tilly belongs to?

And that was the beginning of a beautiful and platonic relationship. We became BFFs. Two chumps who shivered and shuddered through junior high school. I watched her play soccer for the Boys and Girls Club League. She watched me dance. She told me she was Métis and I got it. I told her I was gay and she couldn't care less. I went to her place for venison stew and bannock; she came to mine for poutine and tourtière. A match made in heaven. We held on to each other for dear life and made it through to grade nine.

And then we passed through the portals of high school and things went from bad to worse. It was okay when we could be together, but we took different classes and couldn't always meet during lunch or spares. While I became the object of ridicule and cruelty, Tilly found refuge in the bathroom. Tucked her legs under her arse, locked the cubicle door, and ate her baloney sandwiches in relative, if stinky, peace. Like I said, I had the library.

We both stayed alive. Barely.

But since Ms. McDonald, Tilly has come into her own and is one of the best players. She doesn't have to eat in the can anymore. I'm glad for Tilly. She's been elevated to the tolerable because of her soccer skills. Now that we're in grade twelve we have more chances to hang, just chowing down lunch in front of her locker. But I seldom go into the gym with her. I did once last year, just to watch her practise at lunch time. Then James Mulroney started spitting at me, and I had to leave. So I waited until spring when practice moved outside, and I could better position myself away from any arcs of saliva. Tilly understood. Even though I can't always watch her practise, she knows I completely support her and cheer her on.

Mostly I just run to the studio. It is *my* best refuge. I practise at least five hours a day. Two in the morning before school and three after. And I am there almost all day every Saturday. Dance is a grueling discipline. But I love it.

There are mirrors across the wall. The floor is one of those hardwood sprung types, easier on the knees, but very expensive.

We are always told to respect the floor. There are barres against one wall. Windows across the room for natural light. It really is a beautiful room. The Steinway piano is tucked into a corner. There are other smaller studios, too. But this is the one I like best. Where I hide from the Whitleigh world. Where I danced. Where I dance.

Sometimes I just work at the barre if there is another class going on. But the best is when the studio is empty, which it often is at noon. That's when I am truly free. With music or without. Jeté. Jeté. Leap and turn across the floor. I love to travel at great speed, imagining I am as fast as light. I watch my posture in the mirror. Concentrate on my centre. Spin upwards and land. Strong. Certain.

Let me clear up a common misperception that picks my butt. Male dancers are not effeminate. We do not wear tutus. Our wrists do not flap. We are expected to be assertive, have strong lines, exude confidence and masculinity. We are simply boys and men who dance. Not all of us are gay. In fact, if there weren't such a stigma in this country and the one to the south about men dancing, I'll bet there'd be a whole lot more male dancers—gay and straight. Just look at Russia. At China. At India. Almost anywhere but North America.

Men dance and are celebrated for it.

Anyone who thinks dance is for sissies is an idiot. Dance is incredibly demanding. Athletic. I can kick higher than most black-belts. But I am almost always sore. Some muscle is always hurting or pulled or strained. My feet are punished and already look older than seventeen.

It's the price dancers pay. Dancing makes me feel alive. Anything is possible. I go into a zone where all there is are breath and body. I am intensely aware of everything and nothing all at once. I invent routines. Characters. Assume the great roles of dance: great princes, downtrodden lovers, proud warriors. I feel possessed and often lose track of time. Sometimes I'll be late for Whitleigh classes. English is right after lunch. But I don't care. Because of dance, I understand Hamlet in a way no other kid does.

I have been transported to Denmark in a way they will never be.

Three times on weekdays and on Sundays I set aside time for weight training. It is very important that I build my body mass and strength. Not to mention my aerobic capacity. I have to be able to perform for minutes at a time. I liken it to a hockey shift.

My uncle sometimes takes me to Oilers games. I'm dazzled by the speed of the skaters. The intensity of their activity for the short times they are on ice reminds me of what I do in the dance studio. In hockey, star players are sometimes on ice for much of the game.

That's just like a principal male dancer. He has to be able to dance full out—leaping in dance is like leaping in track and field or gymnastics—it takes immense energy and strength. Dancing full out, even for seven straight minutes or try ten or fifteen, not to mention an entire evening, not to mention lifting the principal ballerina, requires incredible physical training, just like running or skating. Check out National Ballet of Canada principal stars, Guillaume Côté and his real-life romantic partner, Heather Ogden, who take Advil before every performance and who are always exercising and training.

If you think tap or jazz are any easier, watch *West Side Story* sometime. Watch Gregory Hines. Or Gene Kelly. See a *Cirque de Soleil* show.

So I weight train. Use the stair machine. Not for the end of looking like some Frankenstein freak weight trainer. To build strength and endurance.

And yeah. Sometimes I check out the guys. But I'm very careful about it.

Most of the time there's not much to see. Contrary to popular belief.

That's another great heterosexual myth. That all gay guys want a piece of some straight guy's ass.

Nothing could be farther from the truth.

Most gay guys are pretty picky. (Well, this one is.)

Most straight guys don't even have great asses.

Neither do gay guys want to wind up on the end of some straight guy's fist. Or flat on the floor. Or dead and hanging bloodied on a fence in a field.

So I keep my eyes mostly to myself. I've mastered the surreptitious glance. The nonchalant nod. The sneaky squint.

Once in a while there's a little eye candy.

But most often, I wouldn't stop to buy at the confectionary.

Unless, of course, Jess came for his workout.

We worked out together the Wednesday after our big city date. He invited me. Threw a crumpled ball of looseleaf into my open locker at school as I was scrubbing off the latest message someone had scrawled in marker across the front: "cock king."

Kind of a compliment really. Depends how you look at it.

Anyway, I opened the scrunched paper ball and it was an invitation from Jess to weight train together at the local club.

So we did. Just two guys spotting for each other. Using the elliptical exercisers side by side. Sweating. No shenanigans. That's the thing. Gay guys just like to hang out together, like straight guys. It's not always about sex. But that's always where the straight mind goes. Between the sheets. Don't you sometimes wonder why? Like what's up with that? Who's transfixed? Obsessed? And why?

Afterwards, he drove me home. We set up a real date to see a movie on the weekend. The new one with Tom Cruise. We talked about teachers and football and physics. I said I'd help him with his physics homework sometimes. It was all very lovely.

Truth is, that's all I wanted. To talk.

Truth is… well, think of that old Madonna song. You know the one.

I was a little nervous about the whole sex thing.

Ok. A lot nervous.

I mean. I was sure I could manage and all. Don't get me wrong. It's just… well, like any novice, I was anxious. You know. Everyone likes to make a good first impression. What if I sucked (no gross pun intended)?

So. I guess I hoped Jess wasn't in a hurry. I wasn't really ready for that particular dance, is all.

SEVEN

And Then He Kissed Me

My mom and Madame came with me to the BIGGEST AUDITION OF MY LIFE at the Ballet Academy in the city. I hardly slept the night before but managed to eat a decent enough breakfast.

It was a chilly mid-October day. Most of the leaves were gone from the trees as we drove through the streets to our 9 am sharp appointment. We got to the dance academy in plenty of time. A nice, rotund lady checked off my name at the registration table and gave me number 207 to wear for the day. I left Madame and Mom behind in the lobby with the other uptight parents and nail-biting teachers and snivelling siblings and went into the change room.

I nodded to the other boy in the change room. His name was Sergio. I knew him from dance functions. Of course, there were fewer danseurs than danseuses auditioning. That would be true across the country. Although surely there are some potentially fabulous dancers—gay and straight—out there. But the stigma is still so pernicious. What straight guy would risk it as a dancer? So male dancers are always in the minority. But I figured that might work in my favour.

I changed into my black shorts, T-shirt and ballet shoes. Put my street clothes in my gym bag. Pinned the number 207 to my shirt and walked out of the dressing room. Down the hall to the dance studio.

I was here last year for a master class with an instructor from the National Ballet School. Greg Zwidinsky. He was impressed with me and suggested I do the National Ballet School audition the following year—this October. I told him that Madame had that very same idea. Greg was impressed that I was working with Madame.

"So Isadora Branislov ended up here, did she? I always wondered what became of Herself after the fiasco."

I was dying to know more, but I kept my mouth shut and just nodded. That whole rest of the afternoon I felt Greg's eyes on me. Assessing. Before I left, he gave me a few pointers to work on throughout the coming year. This past year.

So much can happen in a year. I danced. I trained. I dreamed.

I fell for a gay guy playing straight.

And now, finally: D DAY! Dance Day. I felt nauseous. Excited. Elated. Terrified.

I opened the double doors to the large, brightly-lit studio. The pianist was warming up with some Chopin études. I crossed the floor to the barre where the ballerina hopefuls—Leonora Pinkowski among them—were busy stretching and balancing. I began to stretch out. The tension at the barre, in the room, was palpable.

At precisely 9 am, the National Ballet instructors clapped their hands and invited us to sit on the hardwood floor.

One instructor, a petite gamine ballerina-type, introduced herself as Sheila Glibbons and the other was the incredibly tall and slim Sara Kimberley. I was a little disheartened that Greg was not present.

"All of you are here because you are already fine dancers at the senior level," Sheila began. "We want you to know from the outset that we appreciate how nervous you must be and how very much you want the opportunity to attend the National Ballet School.

"But you must also know that the National Ballet School can only offer a certain number of positions—one hundred and fifty to be exact—for Stage Two of its auditions. And even fewer—fifty— for the Intensive Dance Program for advanced post-secondary training in the fall. That means most of you will not be attending the school this summer or next fall."

I glanced around at my sister—and fellow—dancers, recognizing that maybe one or two of us would make this audition, if any. It was a sobering thought.

Sara took up the thread. "However, we hope you will view this audition today as a learning experience—like a master class—and not a competitive battlefield or your absolute last chance at ever entering a dance school.

"After all, there are many reputable dance schools in this country—many opportunities out there for those of you who truly feel dance is your calling."

"Sometimes," Sheila continued with a smile, "what you really need is to find the right fit for what it is you do best: perhaps it's modern dance, perhaps teaching or choreography. Dance therapy even."

I sighed. I knew what I wanted to do, had wanted all my life. Probably like everyone else in this room. And in every audition centre across the country. We all wanted to be professional ballet dancers. On big stages. With big and important companies. We dreamed of becoming principals.

"So work hard today. Keep a positive frame of mind. And… if you don't get accepted, try again. Try another school. And above all, keep dancing. Everybody ready? Let's get up and start at the barre."

And the company rose and swept over to the various barres. There were fifteen of us, so we spaced ourselves out and began.

First pliés. Then tendus. Rond de jambe à terre. Grands battements. I concentrated on my breathing. My centre. My straightness of spine. Leg extensions. Turn out.

Next was centre work. We spread out across the wooden dance floor. Resumed our tendus. Grand battements. Again I focused. Entered the zone. As Madame has taught me to do. Tried not to let my mind wander beyond my body and the mirror and the voice of the instructor and the music from the piano. Next we moved to pirouettes—a particular strength of mine. En dehors. En dedant. I could see other dancers in my peripheral vision, but I tried not to let them into my zone. Refused to let myself register that this was a competition and these were my enemies. Tried to see them as a company.

With me as the principal.

I was given the chance to pirouette as soloist.

As I had thousands of times before, I prepared, turned, spotted, turned, spotted, turned, spotted, turned, spotted, turned and finished. Ten revolutions. Repeated the same in the opposite direction.

"Nicely done," Sara said, as I crossed to the side of the classroom.

Sergio, I noted, had terrific lines. He hasn't been dancing as long as I have, but he's got promise.

I was feeling quite warmed up by the time we moved to the allegro. The first involved changement, assemblé and my specialty: grand jeté. So much training—flexibility, aerobic, strength—paid off. As I leapt to my finish, the class applauded. I could feel the rush to my cheeks.

In fact, the rest of the class was a rush. We finished off with a moving allegro, including waltzes and balances and batteries. I saw Sheila watching me closely. Tried not to let it get to my head.

Instead I thought about my lines, my breadth of movement. The elevation in my leaps. I stayed centred.

At the end of the class, Sheila and Sara called us together and thanked us. We'd be hearing from the school after the last of the auditions. We applauded our instructors and the pianist.

I left the room and ran down the hall to Mom and Madame. My hair was a mess and I stank, but I threw my arms around them.

"Ee-an! What? How did you do, my prize?"

"I did everything, everything just as you would have wanted, Madame! I can't believe how I feel. It went so well! I did the best I possibly could have!" I gushed and beamed. She placed a smoky kiss on my cheek and wandered over to Pinkowski.

My mother took the towel from around my neck and dried my dampened hair playfully. Her voice was a little shaky. "I almost took up smoking again with Madame."

"Oh no."

"That woman… she's great, but batty as a loon."

"It's her genius." I looked over at Madame who was talking with Leonora. Madame winked a heavily made-up eye at me. I knew then that I was her favourite.

"You're *my* genius!"

"Ah, Mom…"

And the drive back was magical, even if we were returning to our tight-butt-holed community.

I knew that if I got accepted, my grandparents had offered to pay for my ticket to Toronto for the Summer School—Stage Two Auditions. They would also foot the bill for the tuition, and—gulp—it was huge! I would stay with my aunt Becky who lives in Scarborough.

Then the entire summer would be an audition to see if I would be accepted into the Intensive Dance Program in the fall. It's year-long, advanced post-secondary training for people like me who want to be professional dancers.

Merely the dream of my lifetime.

There is no better school for ballet than the National Ballet School. Everyone in Canada knows this. The whole ballet world knows it.

And everything was going ticketyboom. Until Jess. And that kiss…

After that fateful event, my head which was usually screwed on pretty straight, was not so straight. Which I guess makes sense. Since I'm not straight. Suddenly, I had trouble concentrating. Finding and keeping my centre. So absolutely essential to dance. To becoming a professional.

Instead, I found myself wondering what Jess would think of the dance step I was working on. What would he think of my jeté? Me in this or that dance role or costume? It was ridiculous. Really.

But I couldn't seem to help myself. He flooded my thoughts. And my dreams.

I was obsessed with Jess Campeau.

Me and every straight little perky-breasted she-thing in our embarrassing suburb.

So when the letter came, twelve weeks to the day, Ian Trudeau— yes this very boy—should have received the thrill of his seventeen short years when he was accepted to the National Ballet School summer program.

But what did I think instead?

How would I survive four weeks away from this, my homely little hitherto loathed and hopelessly screwed-up satellite community?

Meaning… how would I survive four weeks—and possibly thereafter a year—without Jess Campeau sucking away my wind and my sense and my sensibility?

EIGHT

All Made Out of Ticky-Tacky

Why do parents make their kids live in the burbs?

Status. If you live in White Oaks. And even if you don't. Every bedroom community has its own version of White Oaks. And envies those who live there. Especially their view of the golf course.

I know my mom moved to our suburb because all those years ago it was the only place she could afford. After my loser father took off. My gramma and grampa helped her. They live here, too. And she had a baby and no life and no job. So she returned to the place she grew up. And now I'm so *blessed* to grow up here, too.

But since my mom's glowing girlhood, this community has gotten so expensive and uppity she could never afford to buy here if she were just starting out. I mean, she can barely afford the taxes. I tried asking her to move to the city. But the house is paid off and is my mom's only investment. Her piano and music theory students are here and she'd lose most, if not all, of them and her only source of income if we moved. At this point in her life, we're still just touching middle class.

How depressing.

When you're an only child of a single mother you get to hear all this stuff, all the parental worries and dreams. My mom has never remarried. She's hardly even gone on a few dates. So I'm her man. Her gay son who understands.

But even though my mom is great, I don't think she sees what I see about living here in Turd Park, as I call it.

Running under the streets, beneath the strip malls, the architecturally controlled, gated neighbourhoods, there's a noxious current swirling under the belly of the beast.

Sometimes in our SPAM club at school or in social studies, Mr. Monaghan talks about the suburb mentality with us. Mr. Monaghan is a cool guy. He's kind of a throwback hippie. His hair is long and he doesn't much go in for fashion. He drives a puke green Volkswagon van. And he is serious about stuff like peace and global warming and the environment and human rights, including gay rights. And he asks us questions about our world and our lives. Makes us think. Demands to know what difference we're going to make.

"What's wrong with the suburbs, Mr. M? I mean, don't you live here, too?" Ken Dropko, just one of many thick-and-red necks who are in my social class, rallied to defend our dudsville.

"Actually, no. I live in the city. But this isn't about me. It's about you, so I open it up to you, class. What's wrong with the suburbs?"

Erika the Goth girl shifted in the desk in front of me. She lives on my very same crescent. I've known her since she wasn't Goth but a ginger-haired kindergarten kid who liked to draw. I don't think she and I have spoken in ten years. But I often follow behind her as she marches off to school in her Goth garb, black hair swinging across her back.

"Suburbs are for spoiled kids and their spoiled parents," Stoner Tim Dwightson, or STD as he's fondly known, offered from his usual place at the back of the room.

"And you're not one of those." Mr. Monaghan's voice was bland.

"Hell, no."

"Everything's the same here," Tammy Ludvig smacked her gum. "Like when I go to my Oma's? In Fort McLeod where she lives? It's like, all the houses and everything? They're like different? Painted different colours and stuff? And they're kinda pretty. And stuff? With front porches and porch swings? Or just like different? Not like here where everybody's house is like one of three shades of beige?"

I looked at Tammy. She's probably a person who admires the artist Pink. Everything about her is pink. Lip gloss. Blush. Magenta leggings to match the streaks in her hair.

"Interesting Tammy. I think you're on to something. There was a song in the sixties…"

The class groaned. Mr. Monaghan was fond of revisiting his golden age.

"No, hear me out. Because this song still has relevance today. In fact, I hear different versions of it on the TV show, *Weeds*. It's a song by Melvina Reynolds called 'Little Boxes.' In the song she critiques the suburbs and their sameness: the houses she equates with boxes, the people who live in the little boxes, the children of the people in the little boxes. All made out of 'ticky tacky.' It's a classic. I'll find it on YouTube and play it for you next day.

"But what can we attribute this sameness to? Why would a whole community opt for sameness?"

I decided to enter the discussion. Everyone in class knows I have strong opinions. I can sense my classmates wincing when I start up. But I can't help myself. I really can't.

"I think it has something to do with money. With privilege. With segregation. With racism. A sense of entitlement. An ignorance of the world beyond the borders."

Erika the Goth girl turned around to glare at me. "Like you've been beyond the borders? We live on the exact same street. Where the hell have you ever traveled beyond Turid Park, Trudeau?"

"Except across the dance floor. Ha ha ha." The class snickered at Ken Dropko's lame-ass joke.

"Enough! Ian's got a point. Between today and Wednesday's class, I want you to observe your community. Really take a look. What do you see? What kinds of people? IS there diversity? Are you and your neighbours made out of 'ticky tacky'?"

The bell rang and I stood to go. But Erika whirled around and her face was fire truck red instead of its usual Goth pallor.

"You think you know it all, don't you, Trudeau? Well, you don't. Just once I'd like to see you go through an entire class *without* talking. Just once I'd like to see *you* listen. You might even learn something. You don't have the answer to *everything*. You live here with the rest of us. Don't be such a freaking hypocrite!" And she stormed past me and out the door.

I was shocked.

I gathered my books and swallowed the hurt that was welling up in my throat. What did I ever do to Erika? Why did she spit this venom at me?

And was it true what she said?

The rest of the day I kept returning to her words. Honestly, I wanted to go into the can and cry. But that would make me a fag.

So I didn't.

Instead I tried to concentrate on my social teacher's homework assignment. I wanted to defend myself. Gather enough proof to prove Erika wrong. I may not have travelled, but I know where she and I live. And it ain't pretty.

In the past few years, especially since I entered the golden age of gay adolescence, I have been really looking at this suburban paradise that is my forced place of residence.

We don't have homeless people wandering around to dirty up our streets, but there sure are a lot of people lined up at the food bank. Or down at the Salvation Army soup kitchen. And we sure seem to love our six-and nine-foot fences around our properties and our thousands of dollars security systems to keep out all the non-existent criminals.

We have every amenity that the large city offers, but few small independent businesses stand a chance here. City developers intend to landfill the nearby wetlands, but thank goodness for our two pristine golf courses.

Did I mention that our women's shelter is full to overflowing?

Or that in about an hour I can find out where you can get your heroin or crystal meth fix?

The façade of our suburb is the façade in our school. By all surface appearances, a nice school. Nice teachers. Nice administrators. Nice, nice students.

So very lonely.

NINE

All the Lonely People, Where Do They All Come From?

"**I**'m not lonely." Jess was clicking his pen in time to the Maroon 5 song on the radio.

"Never?"

"Naw."

I shrugged. "Lucky you. You're a jock. No one even remotely suspects you're gay. You're part of the mainstream. Congratulations." I turned back to my physics.

"Ok. Some… sometimes I feel, you know. A little lost."

"Around McDade and your other jock buddies?"

"Sometimes. But," he grinned, "we can have fun together, too. A lot of fun. Just doing stupid stuff. Playing pool. Wii games. Getting drunk and running around the golf course after dark. Replaying great football or hockey games in our heads."

"Talking about chicks."

"Yeah… that, too."

"Don't you feel like a hypocrite?" I heard the words reverberate in my head from Erika's accusation.

"What am I supposed to do, Ian? I'm not you. I'm not 'out.' And I can't ever be. Sometimes you're so s–s–s…"

"Sanctimonious? Self-righteous?"

"Yeah. Both of those. Who died and made you god, anyways?"

Shit. Twice in one day.

I guess I *do* have a strong streak of self-righteousness. It comes of my work in SPAM. My mom and I volunteering at the women's shelter. It comes from washing shit about me, the flaming queer, off my locker every other week. I get full of myself. How revolting.

But is it so very bad to care? To want the world to change? To want to change the world?

"Sorry, Jess. I know it's tough for you, too."

"Yeah," he said softly. "But it's true. Until you, I never really thought about how hard it is for other people who aren't... you know cool."

I wondered if I should tell him the story. I didn't want to sound like some kind of preaching saint again. I took a sip of Coke and began slowly.

"So there's this girl I know. Not Tilly. But related to her. Okay. Her younger sister, Régine. She used to go to Whitleigh with us at the start of the year. Now she goes to the storefront school at the local mall, right next to SportChek."

"Is Whitleigh really that bad?" Jess continued to play with his mechanical pencil.

I shifted position at the dining room table. Closed my physics text. Looked him square in the eyes. "Judge for yourself after the story. Régine was in French 9 class when she got the note."

"Note?"

"Uh huh. A note. Consisting of ten words accompanied by a picture. A naked girl getting screwed from behind by one guy and another guy with his dick in her mouth. The caption: 'This is what we'd like to do to you, bitch.'"

"What kind of scumbag...?"

I didn't point out that these were exactly the kinds of scumbags Jess hung out with. "Régine was frantic when she caught up to Tilly and me and showed it to us. We took her to the French teacher, Madame Le Clerc. She got upset and turned it in to the administration."

"What happened?" Jess leaned over his homework.

"Nothing happened."

"Nothing?"

"Nada. We waited all day. For Régine to be called to the office. For the person or persons responsible to be apprehended. Le Clerc checked in at the office several times. She'd narrowed down the handwriting to some boys in the same class as Régine and let the administration know."

"What'd Kato say?" Jess looked stunned.

"Kato!" I felt my mouth pucker in disgust. "Kato said nothing. Did nothing. Régine was a wreck at the end of the day. She clung to Tilly and me. Too terrified to walk home. Terrified to stay in the building. So Le Clerc drove us all home.

"Tilly and I wanted to tell Mrs. Monpetit, her mom, about the incident—Mr. Monpetit works up north and was out of town at the time—but Régine made us promise not to."

"Why the hell not?"

"I still don't understand why not. But think about it. I figure she felt like she was the filthy one. I mean, somehow that note dirtied and sullied Régine in her own eyes. Guess that's what that kind of stuff does.

"Anyway, I fumed about it all night. I wanted to tell my mom, too, but I didn't. It almost killed me to keep all that shit inside. I hardly slept. Tilly either. The next day, Régine pretended to be sick and wouldn't go to school. So Tilly and I went to see Kato that morning. We brought along Madame Le Clerc as our trustworthy adult."

"And?"

"And again… nothing. Kato went on and on about how these were troubled boys who'd come a long way. Needed another chance. Were sorry. All that crap. Tilly just sat there with tears welling up. Le Clerc seemed stunned by the whole thing. Finally, I kind of lost it and blurted out, 'What about Régine in all this? She's scared to even come to school. Isn't school supposed to be a safe and caring place? Isn't that what Whitleigh brags its ass about all the time? What kind of safety are you offering to a grade nine girl who gets a porn note delivered to her? What about Régine?'"

Jess's eyes widened. "And Kato said...?"

"He said, and I quote, 'Oh, Régine. She's a little doll.' A frigging doll? Can you believe it? I almost choked. 'She's not a doll. She's a person! A frightened girl! A girl who's been sexually harassed!'"

"You said that to the principal?" A note of admiration crept into Jess's voice.

"Yeah. And I said, 'What are you going to do to the guys who did this to her? How are you going to make sure Régine gets to and from school safely?'"

"Then what?"

"Then there was a lot of throat clearing and fat jowl shaking and sniffing, hemming and hawing, telling us about verbal reprimands given to the offenders that amounted to nothing. He didn't even call Mrs. Monpetit. Never intended to. And he finished off with an advisory for me to watch my tone."

"You called him on it and he took offence."

"Yup." I swallowed the last of my pop. "But I felt so bad for Tilly. She was just so shocked, you know. She really believed, I guess we all did, that Kato would do something on her sister's behalf. But he was really siding with the guys who'd sent the note. And I felt like puking."

"Shit."

"No shit." We sat in silence for a few seconds. "But you know what the terrible irony was, Jess?"

"What?"

"That conversation was two days before the December 6th vigil. You know, the one organized by some staff and students every year? We commemorate the victims of the Montreal massacre at l'École Polytechnique in 1989..."

"I've never been..."

"Every year we light candles in the gym. Every year we remember the young women who died at that school. Every year we remember other victims of violence—women, girls, boys, men—throughout the country and the world. Like my mom who was in an abusive marriage. Like Matthew Shepard. And every year Kato is invited but never attends.

"After the conference in the office, I couldn't get over the fact that a principal of a high school could be that thick. That insensitive. And then I overheard him in the hallway a day later and that was it. I knew I had to do something."

"What'd you hear?

"Exactly a day before the vigil and a day after we appealed on Régine's behalf to him, he says about the vigil, 'Fucking feminists and their fucking vigil!'"

"No way! He said that out loud?"

"He was talking privately to the vice-principal. He didn't see me standing nearby. But I overheard it, loud and clear. And I made a decision on the spot."

"To do what?"

"To call the newspaper and tell them what kind of man was in charge of Whitleigh."

"Hey! I remember that! I read that piece in the *Herald Weekly*. You were the anonymous tipster?"

"Yup." I got up from the table. Moved over to our living room sofa. Jess followed me.

"Shit, Ian!"

"I told the reporter everything. About the note. About Régine. About the school's refusal to do anything on her behalf. About the vigil and Kato never attending. About Kato's stupid, asinine remark."

Jess whistled. "Incredible! So they printed it and the shit hit the fan?"

"Sort of. Kato and Vice-Principal Brice back-pedaled like mad. Phoned up Mrs. Monpetit immediately after the story broke. Told her they'd had every intention of calling her. Suspended the two guys for a week. Made them write Régine a letter of apology.

"But Mrs. Monpetit pulled Régine out of school. As a grade nine girl in a school of 1200 people and two particular asswipes, she just didn't feel safe. It was all too little, too late. Can you blame her?"

"Guess not. So what happened next to Kato and Mr. Brice?"

"Nothing."

"Huh?"

"No repercussions. They went on their good-old-boy administrative way. Told the follow-up reporter from the *Herald* that they'd make a point of attending the vigil in the future. No harm was intended. They never meant to slight the student organizers. Denied flatly the anti-feminist remark. Insisted that the incident with the male students had been settled. And everyone lived HEA."

"HEA?"

"Happily ever after. Except, of course, for Régine. She won't be attending Whitleigh. Or graduating with her classmates. She goes to the Learning Centre."

"That's screwed."

"Yeah. Every once in a while she talks about attending the other high school. Maybe it would be better there."

"Maybe." Jess took a swig of his Coke. "How come you're so together about everything?" He turned his body and looked directly at me.

I blushed. "I'm not really."

"Sure as hell are."

I thought about it. So many times I used avoidance as a tactic. I was afraid of certain guys in the school. Certain places. I stuck close to Tilly. To the studio. To home. How together was that? But I had the benefits of a great friend, my grandparents, my mother.

"My mom... I guess. She's the one, the example. A single parent who left a brute of a husband when I was a baby. She raised me to stick up for myself. To think for myself. To care about people. She volunteers at the women's shelter and at the Bissell Centre and she sometimes drags me along with her. And she thinks I'm terrific. And tells me that. Like almost everyday."

"Wow. Must be nice."

I smiled. Even though Mom sometimes goes overboard with the safe sex and pro-gay mom routine, she is pretty great. "Yeah. It is."

Jess shook his head. "Shit. Who knew? About Kato? About Whitleigh?"

"C'mon, Jess. You knew. You know."

"Yeah... guess I did. And do."

"It's why we're only friends after dark. After school."

He put his arm around me. "Is that what we are? Friends?"

My heart was pounding madly. "I dunno... I think so."

"I think more than friends, Ian."

I caught my breath.

"There won't be any more crap written on your locker, okay?"

"Can you make that happen?"

"Pretty sure."

"Thanks Jess."

"You're pretty frigging brave, Ian." His amazing eyes had me dazed. I felt like a deer in headlights.

"Didn't make any difference in the end, did it?"

"Does to me, Ian." And he kissed me.

And suddenly I felt very brave.

But that ended Wednesday when I walked into social class and met the death stare of Erika the Goth girl.

Throughout social class the debate continued about our ticky tacky suburb. Most of the students had done their homework.

Some slagged our community.

But most celebrated our neighbourhoods: the block parties, the charity drives, the seniors' residence with paved walking trails, bike paths, neighbourhood watches, snow removal services, carpooling and park-and-ride services, community recycling and composting campaigns, the quick and easy access to amenities and emergency services.

Still others praised Whitleigh for being a public, state-of-the-art school that opened its doors to all, regardless of class or colour or religion. Even if there isn't much diversity in the student population, the school would never turn away anyone from the community who wished to attend.

And Erika finished off the discussion with a summary of the diversity of our very own Oriole Crescent. She'd done her research. Managed to take a poll, though I don't know who would have answered the door to someone who looks as though she'd crawled from the crypt and only comes out after nightfall. But then again, she's lived on our street at least as long as I have. Apparently, we have a Jewish family, a secular Muslim family, a number of

Ukrainian-Canadians, German-Canadians, and a mixed-race family living along good ol' Oriole. She turned around to smirk darkly at me.

And I, Ian Trudeau, never said a word.

TEN
Silence is Golden

True to Jess's word, the nasty graffiti evaporated from my life. Well... at least my locker. Sniggering remarks, just within earshot, persisted.

One day, I overheard McDade and Greene talking to Cathy Simco, president of the grad committee.

"Hey. Why don'tcha get Trudeau to help with grad decorations. He's a fag. All fags are artistic!"

Even more humiliating, Cathy took their advice and did ask me. I turned her down.

"Why, Ian? It's your grad, too." Tilly was painting her toenails while I flipped through a celebrity magazine and we listened to Beyoncé. We'd been arguing over who was hotter—elf boy, Orlando Bloom (Tilly's pick), vampire boy, Robert Pattinson (tied between us—literally or metaphorically), or geezer babe, Johnny Depp (my favourite by a mile).

"Mathilde Monpetit! You know very well that I don't have a visual art bone in my body."

"That's not what Jess says."

"Shut-up. We haven't done anything. Much anyway. And you know what I mean, Tilly. Everyone thinks gay guys all have the gay aesthetic. Just like all black guys have rhythm."

"Like all Indians drum and dance or do beadwork."

I laughed. Tilly hated sewing. She'd almost flunked Home Ec in junior high.

"Or all Métis play the fiddle and step dance. Except that my moshum really does."

"Yeah, well. Gregory Hines—black *and* straight—*was* a great dancer. And Carson on *Queer Eye* is a Fashion Savant. But I still can't draw, cut, design or make poofy table centrepieces to save my gay life. I could, however, dance about each table and sprinkle good luck grad sparkles everywhere. That would go over big."

We laughed.

"Seriously. What are you going to do about grad?"

"Well, since Jess isn't about to ask me for obvious reasons - I'm going with you."

"I've been meaning to talk to you about that."

"Tilly… we promised each other years ago…"

"That if no one hot asked either of us, we'd go to grad together…"

"So?"

"So it happened."

"Someone hot asked you to grad?"

"Don't sound so surprised, Ian!" She threw a pillow at me. "Yes, as a matter of fact. There's this guy. Howie Strathern."

"Howie Strathern! Howie-the-track-star-running-genius-who-can't-string-a-full-sentence-together Strathern?"

Tilly looked hurt. There it was again: my big smartass mouth. "I mean, sure, Howie. He's pretty good looking." At six-foot-five, and about 170 pounds he'd look like a skinny version of André the Giant beside her. "Yeah. Cool."

"Ian. I like him. He's not smart like you, but he's the first guy—the first straight guy—who's ever taken an interest in me. Ever! I'd like to go to grad with him. Even if he's a little, okay a lot socially awkward. You'll still be there. To help ease the uncomfortable silences."

"I guess."

Tilly took my hand. "I can see that you're disappointed. But Jess will be there. Maybe, just maybe…"

"What? We'll dance? Get crowned the Whitleigh Grad Queen and Queen? What are you thinking, Tilly?" I slumped down on the floor, feeling sorry for myself. Grad would be utterly meaningless for me. I was dreading it. And now Tilly was telling the gay loser that she had other grad plans.

"Hey, Ian." Tilly voice was a caress. "It's only February. Lots can happen between now and May. You never know."

"Yeah, I guess you never do. Know." That word was sure hovering around my brain lately, almost as much as Jess Campeau. Already feeling grad-glum, I thought I'd share Erika the Goth's recent accusation with my best friend. Get a little perspective. Even if the truth might hurt. "Hey, Tilly. I was wondering about something." I told her about the incident in social. "What do you think, Tillster? Am I that guy? The one who doesn't shut-up to listen? Who knows it all?"

"Well…" Tilly concentrated on the appliqué she was applying to her big toenail. "It's not like you're a bad friend who never listens to me or my problems."

"Uh-huh."

"But there's a kernel of truth to that other part." She avoided my gaze.

"Shitacular." I hugged my knees and buried my head.

"Look," Tilly's soft voice again. "You're a great person, Ian. You care about all the right stuff. I love you no matter what. Here's what my moshum says: we learn all kinds of things, find solutions to problems even, by being quiet. By just listening. To nature. To each other. To the world around us." She touched my arm, since I wasn't looking at her. "Let's try it for a few minutes."

So Tilly switched off the tunes. And we just sat there in her little cramped and cluttered bedroom. Listening.

What did I hear? Mrs. Monpetit sizzling something over the stove. The bark of Beau, the family's black lab, in the back yard. The hum of some passing car. And that white noise of electric currents in the house. Our breathing. The whisper of my own conscience.

Tilly broke the stillness. "That was cool."

"Yeah." I smiled at her. "But…Tilly, I-I… want to change the world."

"We all want to change the world, Ian."

"Can being still, can silence change the world, Tilly?"

"You never know."

No I didn't know.

I felt less and less sure about anything. About myself. About grad. About this queer all-consuming relationship with Jess.

So I asked him as we sat in his car after a movie. "Will you go to grad with me?"

"'Scuse me?"

"I mean not hold hands and stuff. Just kind of… sit together."

"Are you out of your flippin' mind, Trudeau?"

"I guess."

He saw that I was pretty hurt by his tone. "Look. My parents will be there. My father."

"You said they weren't coming to the banquet."

"Still. The whole school would… see us. Together."

"We'd just be two friends."

"No one knows you're… my *friend*, Ian. No one knows."

"And you couldn't stand it if they did. At the very end of your high school life."

"There'd still be a month left of school. How would I survive?"

"You'd survive."

"Not my father. Not when he found out."

"You could leave home."

"And go where?"

I knew it was a stupid idea. A gay boy's pipe dream. Like somehow Jess could stay with Mom and me. Somehow manage to keep a life going. At barely eighteen. Without his parents. "Fine. I just thought I'd ask."

"I'm going with Brittany Westlock. I've already asked her. And that's that."

"I said fine."

"Look, Ian." He smiled weakly. "I'll find you at aftergrad."

"What? And have your way with me in the woods? What if the boys stumble across us?"

He sobered. "I can't be… Ian… I just can't be gay."

ELEVEN
Freak Out

At thirteen I sat my mother, Suzette Trudeau, down. It was my big coming out moment. I'd returned home from summer dance camp, where I'd kissed a boy. I wanted to tell her that I was different. That I felt like a freak. That she would never attend my wedding. Well, not my straight wedding, anyway. I took a deep breath.

"Ian, I know."

"Huh?"

"I know, honey."

"You know what?"

She sighed. "That you're gay."

"I am? I mean… I am."

"Good, then. We both know."

"How did you?"

"I've always known."

"How?"

"A mother knows these things."

"Not all mothers…"

"Well, this one."

I thought about my early aptitude for dance. My admiration for Cher. Jann Arden. Celine Dion. *Queer Eye for the Straight Guy. So You Think You Can Dance.* In some ways, I'm a walking stereotype.

"What about Gramma and Grampa?"

"They know, too. I told them when you were still very young that I thought you might be gay."

"But Mom! They'll hate me."

"No, Ian. They won't. They will always love you. Like I do. You know they understand. Especially Grampa."

"He does?"

"Grampa had a younger brother, Léon."

"Léon? I've never heard of him."

"He's dead."

"How'd he die?"

"Léon hanged himself, Ian."

"He did? Why?"

"Think about it, hon. Why would a man of your grandfather's generation hang himself?"

I covered my face with my hands. "Because he was gay."

"Léon never told anyone, but your grampa knew. In his bones. The way I did. Grampa loved Léon—he was his favourite of four brothers. He never got over his death, really."

I thought about that. About a world that drove a young man to take his life. Simply because he loved other men. Half a century separates me from my Great-uncle Léon. And still young men take their lives for the same reason.

"And Ian?"

I peeked through my fingers at my mother.

"You're not a freak of nature. No matter what anyone may say about or write about or spit at you. You are a wonderful young man. An incredibly talented, bright, sometimes too mouthy but still lovable young man. Who happens to be gay."

We were both tearing up by now. She got up quickly from the kitchen table where our adult coffee cups were sitting in attendance at this very adult conversation that I had initiated but that had somehow gotten away from me. I hated coffee. But I took a sip anyway.

And then Suzette Trudeau, my very own mother, came back with a shoebox. Full of pamphlets. All about sex. How to use a condom. STDs and the risks for homosexual men. GLBT information and website listings. A rainbow flag and buttons. All kinds of stuff that no mother should know about.

"Listen, here's a card for the local youth support group. And this is a program from a very excellent speaker I went to hear. This is a brochure about self-care and making good choices. And…"

"Enough! Mom! This is too much. I just wanted you to know."

"So do I, Ian. And I want you to know. A lot. About the risks. About the people out there who are for you. And against you. So that you can be safe. I want you to *know*."

"Fine. Fine. I'll read this. It's just weirding me out that you have all this. You're kind of… well… like Super Fag Mom, or something."

"Hey, I should get a T-shirt!"

"A cape is more likely!"

"I could wear it to our next parent-teacher interview."

"And on your way to the school you could fight gay-hate crimes and rid the world of white supremacists."

"Hey! Great idea! And you could be my sidekick son!"

"The Queerinator!"

"It's got a ring to it!"

So my great coming out was trumped by my own mother. But I have to say that I felt immense relief, too. I mean, I guess I sort of knew she knew. But to say it out loud—ok she said it out loud first—and not have her turn on me or disown me or think I was some monster… well that was pretty cool. Even if she still bugs me about safe sex and gives me condoms in my Christmas stocking and leaves gay literature around the house in a most embarrassing way. It could sure be worse. Like it was for Jess.

His father was over in Afghanistan, due home in April. So Jess was feeling a little reprieve from the homophobic cloud that descended upon the family home when his dad was around.

"He calls us a bunch of poleriders, f-ing bum punchers, dicklickers, pedophiles, freaks, bum buddy bastards…"

"Wow. He sounds a little obsessed, Jess."

"You think?"

"Think he's afraid of something?"

"Like his kid, his only male heir, being gay?"

"Yeah. That and maybe that he's gay, too, and someone will figure it out if he doesn't pose as virulently anti-gay?"

"My dad? Naw. He's in the military."

"So? We're everywhere. Gays are in the military, Jess. Remember: Don't ask. Don't tell—from the Clinton administration? That sure as heck spilled over our borders!"

"I know but… he's my dad. He's a pretty straight guy."

"As far as you know…"

We turned back to our homework.

"Guess you'll never invite me over to your house to work on physics, hey Jess?"

"Guess not." Jess toyed with his mechanical pencil. "He caught me once. With a friend. We were only little boys. Grade three or four at the most. Experimenting. I thought my dad was gonna pop a vein. My friend took off."

"What'd your dad do?"

"Threw me down the stairs. Broke my arm."

"Shit, Jess! Didn't anyone say anything? Where was your mom? Didn't the doctors ask questions?"

Jess shook his head. "My mom was out in the garden. Kids fall down and break their arms all the time. I knew enough to keep my mouth shut."

"I'm so sorry, Jess." I touched his arm. No wonder he's scared into the closet with a dad like that. Maybe Jess'll be in there for life...

"For a long time, I played very safe. Still do. Until you, that is." He smiled weakly.

"So when did you realize... you know... that you were... gay?"

His voice was miserable. "I couldn't get these images out of my mind. I just... can't. Especially since junior high." He banged the table with his fist. "I'm so freaking screwed up. Why can't I just be normal?"

"Jess. Jess. We are fine the way we are. You're not screwed up. Your dad's the one with the big problem."

"I'm... I'm... a fucking mistake. A freak of nature."

"No, Jess. You're not."

"Seems lately I'm only happy when I'm around you, Ian. I mean I love sports and everything. I like the straight guys I hang with in football and hockey. But it's such a big lie, you know. I'm so tired of the lying. The game-playing. I hate my life."

I tried to console him. He buried his head in his arms. I stroked his shoulders. His hair. I couldn't think of anything to say except to tell him that I was there for him.

"If he ever finds out, Ian, I'm dead."

Homophobia is so gay.

TWELVE
Even Educated Fleas Do It

When your mom is out of town for the weekend visiting your
aunt...

When you're too old to stay at your grandparents'...

When you're all caught up on your homework... well, almost
caught up...

When you have the night off work...

When finally, finally you are permitted to be home alone for
the first time in your entire seventeen years of existence...

What is a gay boy in love to do?

Did I say love?

Getting ahead of myself.

Jess rang the doorbell at 8:30 pm. I had the music on—Rufus
Wainwright—the candles lit. I'd made popcorn and set out some
bowls of chips. Miss Vicky's.

It was damned romantic. If I do say so myself.

I was so nervous I tripped over the runner on the way to the
door. My palm stuck to the doorknob. Classy.

He'd brought beer. Bootlegged by an older teammate. I took
his jacket.

He was so good-looking, so damned nonchalant, my stomach was doing pirouettes.

I had spent the better part of the day showering, powdering, shaving my ten what-pass-for whiskers, cologning, coifing, re-coifing and making frantic wardrobe selections and last-moment reconsiderations. Jess probably had taken a five-minute shower, dragged a comb through his wet hair and thrown on his jeans and a sweater.

"This you?" he picked up the photo of me in my first dance recital as Autumn, the fall-master.

"You've seen that before."

"Never noticed it."

"Probably because I had it turned to the wall."

"Weren't you the little lord of the dance!" He smirked and I wanted to slam my lips against his. But I didn't. Like I said, I'm a shy guy. About this stuff. Shy and nervous.

We sat on the couch with our beer and made small talk. He talked about his hockey practice. A lot about football. I told him that I didn't understand football all that well. So he tried to explain the intricacies of the game to me and I lamely tried to follow, but all I could think about was how his hands have these great tendons, great definition, like I imagined a sculptor's hands might look. I watched his lips move and heard sounds come out, but it was the way his mouth kind of curved up on the left that kept my attention.

Then Jess stopped talking about football and looked at me. I mean really looked at me. "Tell me about dance."

"What do you want to know?"

"Well, why dance? Why not gymnastics? Or track?"

A Jason Mraz track came on at just that moment. An upbeat, funky rhythm.

"I guess because of the music. I guess because I love to move —to music. Since I was a little tyke. I couldn't help myself… when my mom played piano or the stereo. I was always dancing. And I've devoted so much time to the discipline that it's a part of me. I can't imagine my life without dance, probably like you can't imagine your life without sports—hockey, football. I really think I was born to dance. Like some are born to swim. To climb mountains."

"What are you going to do? I mean, after high school."

I was surprised that he didn't know. That he didn't know this very important thing about me. "I'm going to dance, Jess. I'm training and will continue to train to be a professional dancer. I auditioned for the National Ballet School earlier this fall and I've been invited to the second round of auditions this summer. If I do well—and I intend to do very well—I'll begin the professional program next September in Toronto."

"Toronto?" his voice rose slightly. "You mean you'll be leaving?" And then Jess Campeau, Mr. Smooth, took my hand and brought my palm up to his mouth. "Where will that leave me?"

"I… I don't… know." I had difficulty suddenly forming a coherent thought.

Then he locked his fingers with mine.

"Here. I guess you'll be here while I'm there." My voice was shaky. "You told me that you were going to college in the city. Aren't you?"

"Yeah." And very gently he began squeezing my hand, my fingers. "I guess we'll have to make up for all that lost time, then."

I swallowed, then croaked, "Yeah, I guess."

The track switched to Damien Rice. "The Blower's Daughter."

I can't take my eyes off of you, Damien sang, quite oblivious to the synchronicity of his lyrics.

"Hey, I love this song. Can you dance to this song, Ian?"

"Yeah. I could… I can."

"Show me."

I resisted. Jess tried to get me to stand up.

"I'll feel stupid dancing. Alone."

"Isn't that what you do?"

"No… Sometimes. In rehearsal. In performance, seldom. I dance with a ballerina. Or the company. Rarely solo. Yet. Anyways."

"Why? Why can't you? Dance for me? Just for me?"

"Wow. I mean. It's kind of… you know. Intimate."

"You don't wanna… be intimate with me, Ian?"

"That's not… I…"

"Dance for me, Ian. C'mon. Please. Just this once."

His eyes were too perfect to resist. I stood. Pushed the coffee table out of the way. And I danced. Nothing too theatrical or gymnastic. But I showed Jess me. I showed him Ian. The way I can turn and be perfectly centred. The way my arms extend in desire. The way I isolate the muscles in my torso. My stomach. The strength in my thighs. My back. The flexibility of my legs. And the way my body moves to rhythm and music and the life, the pulse of music. I improvised and I let go. I took a chance. For him.

I finished on my knees, head raised, face up towards the ceiling. Eyes closed.

Jess clapped and whistled. I blushed and rose from the floor. Out of breath. Sweaty. Not just from the dancing. Then he was beside me. Very near me.

"Show me," Jess breathed in my ear. "Show me how to dance."

And so, in a forbidden coupling, behind closed curtains, in my modest house, my neck-craning, ultra-conservative suburban hell turned for a time into a kind of heaven.

I taught him the foxtrot first, because my mom had shown me that one. Then I put on some Duke Ellington and showed him the jitterbug of my grandparents' generation.

And then the slow songs started. Continuing until very late in the night.

I won't tell what happened because I am, after all, a gentleman. And it's no one's business anyway.

But I will say that if Jess Campeau had asked me to give up dancing and stay with him... on that night, I would have. In a heartbeat.

THIRTEEN

A Really Bad Song from the Seventies by 10cc

"Ian?"

"Yeah, Mom?"

"Anything you want to tell me, sonshine?"

I hate when she calls me that. "Like what?" I focused very hard on my English homework—a poster project on gender stereotypes in the media—and tried to will the colour from my cheeks.

"Who's Jess?"

I felt the colour now creeping to my ears.

"Who, Mom?"

"The boy. Jess. Your friend."

I fumbled. "Um, he's just the guy I've been tutoring for months now."

"You mean pretending to tutor."

How did she know? I'd cleaned up. The house was spotless when she returned from my aunt's house. That was it! Too spotless! Like I was covering up the scene of a crime! Which Jess and I weren't. And she would get that. Understand. But she probably knew. About everything. In her insidious mother-of-a-queer way.

My pencil lead broke. Which necessitated my looking for the pencil sharpener. Which I noticed was in her left hand. So I had to finally look up at her standing next to the kitchen table.

"His full name?" In that tone. You know the one.

"Jess Campeau." I let that slide into her brain.

"Francophone. From here?" She meant our charming suburb. I could tell she was checking her memory banks to see if she knew the family or had gone to school with a Campeau.

"No. He's an army brat."

"Oh."

"Can I have the sharpener, please?"

"How serious is this, Ian?"

"It's not. Just casual."

"Are you lying to your mother…?"

"No."

"Because I just wondered why his name is scrawled all over the pages of this scribbler I found in the recycle bin." She produced my thin Hilroy scribbler from behind her back.

Shit. I knew then that I should have burned the bloody thing. "I- I had to destroy it."

"By recycling it?"

"No, I should have shredded it or something."

"Are you hiding something from me?"

I sighed. "No. Just from the crummy world. And the student population of witless Whitleigh."

"Uh huh." She sat down. My hopes were dashed for an abbreviated discussion.

"He's straight. You're in love with a straight boy?"

"I—I'm not in love. And he's not straight. He plays straight. So he won't get beat up by his jock friends or his homophobic father!"

"I see." She set the scribbler down on the table. "How sad."

"Yeah."

"That you're not in love. And that you have to hide not loving him from the world."

She was playing the infamous trap-Ian-in-the-mother-web-of-words trick. I knew I had to tread carefully. "Yeah."

"I hope that—even though you're not in love—you are playing it safe in the sex department."

"MOM!"

"Are you?"

"Am I what?"

"Playing it safe?"

"Is that really any of your business?"

"Until you're eighteen. Yes. And beyond, as a matter of fact. It's in my parental contract. I get to worry about you until the day I die."

She can make me so mad. I just glared at her. Minutes ticked by. I lost the showdown. "Yesssss," I gritted my teeth, "I am playing it safe."

"Good then," she spoke lightly. "I'll give this back to you," she handed me the scribbler, "since you're not in love."

"I need the sharpener, too."

"No, you don't."

"WHAT?" She was really pissing me off.

"Since you're already fifteen minutes late for work."

"SHIT!"

I was. Late. Again. I'd been late for work almost every shift that week. And late for class. Late getting home. I couldn't seem to get my head back into real time. Since… but that was just dumb. I needed to snap out of it.

I worked at the dance studio three days a week. When I wasn't answering phones at the desk, I was either at the barre or dancing.

Every spare minute outside of regular school, preparing for National Ballet School. Ever since I got the letter that they wanted me for the summer program, Madame commanded me.

Dominated my practices. Spied on my exercises. Critiqued my routines. Even brought in male dancers as guest teachers from the provincial ballet company to work with me. Because I was, after all, her prize.

"Ee-an." Today her voice was frosty when she greeted me over the speakerphone.

"Yes, Madame."

"Come into my office, Ee-an."

I shivered as I walked the few paces down the hall to the broom closet she called her office. I knocked once.

"Entrez."

And entrez I did. The usual motes of dust and ash fluttered about in the half-light coming through the venetian blinds. Photographs of Madame as a young principal ballerina adorned the walls. I could smell the remnants of one of her acrid cigarettes. I knew Madame smoked in this office. And more. I suspected her of illicit liaisons. The Ukrainian custodian spoke Russian. But I had no real proof.

"Ee-an." Madame looked across the piles of papers on her unkempt desk. "Sit."

"Yes, Madame."

"I saw you running across icy field. Today. Yesterday."

"Yes… I'm sorry. I was late, Madame."

"Again." She fixed me with her heavily made-up eyes. I felt myself spinning into their vortex. "Three times this week, twice last week, da?"

"Yes, Madame. I- I'm sorry. It's my grade twelve year. I have so much homework…"

She waved away my lie with a beringed hand. "Be good boy. Don't hurting yourself on ice. And above all, Ee-an…" Fascinated, I watched her elaborate ritual of opening her silver case, selecting and lighting a cigarette with her elegant silver lighter.

"Yes, Madame."

Smoke puffed dragon-like from her large Russian nostrils. "Ee-an, you must to promise Madame, don't hurting your heart in love."

"O-ok. Madame." How did she… how could she know? Had she spoken to my mother? Had the two of them discussed me as I ran to the studio?

She leaned forward in her chair. "I being seeing something lately. In your eyes, Ee-an."

"No. Madame. No love."

"No? But something with heart, da?"

"Well, maybe…" I swear her gaze is like truth serum. I couldn't tear my eyes from hers.

"Ee-an! No! This I forbid! You cannot do both! Dancing. Loving. Not now. Maybe not never."

Her smoky voice seemed laced with something deadly. And Madame can be deadly. Especially when she is deadly serious. Which she was.

I felt my sphincter crawl up inside of me. Followed closely by my scrotum.

"To dance is to love, no?"

"No. I mean. Yes, Madame."

"Yes, my prize. Do you know what you want most of all in this inglorious life?" She reached across her desk, pulled my chin close to her face. Her red nails, claws really, threatened to pierce my skin. "Do you, Ee-an?"

I heard Satie float through the walls of Studio A. "Gymnopédie." One of my favourite pieces. I swallowed.

"To dance, Madame." I said simply. "I love to dance."

"Gooood boy. Now back to desk working, my prize. Madame has so many calls to return. And such the headache." She put her hand to her temple.

As I closed the door I saw her swagger to the corner coat rack and reach beneath her cape for the flask of vodka I knew was hidden in the folds.

Chastised, I returned to my clerical duties and managed to get matters mostly caught up for Madame. I didn't think about Jess. Well, hardly thought about him.

Until he called my house late that night. And we talked until two in the morning. When I fell asleep. Until I woke up with the phone in my hand. Late for school.

FOURTEEN
Game's Pain

"**F**ourth down? I thought you said there were only three."

"That's Canadian football. The CFL. This is American. We're watching *NFL Classics*."

"Oh." I tried to focus my attention on the TV screen rather than on Jess's bicep. "Hey! He just went offside!"

"Out of bounds. The kind of offside you mean is mostly in hockey. And soccer." Jess smiled indulgently at me. And at that precise moment I couldn't have cared less. About offside or out of bounds.

He leaned forward now, intent again on the game. I tried to concentrate. But I found my mind wandering up and away from TSN to two nights previous.

We'd found yet another time to be alone together at my house. It's amazing how you can find such occasions, if you set your mind to it. I'd finished rehearsal for the night, and Mom had to go over to Gramma and Grampa's house to work on her taxes. She has a small if not terribly profitable business. So taxes are a complicated and lengthy process. Grampa always helps her. And that left me with the place to myself. In a quick suburban minute I had Jess on his way over.

Things were getting, you know… intense.

And then I blurted something out without thinking.

You know. The words. Those few particular ones that a boy in any straight white-picket suburb should never admit or utter to another boy in that same burb. Especially a boy like Jess Campeau. Popular. Jock supreme. Buddy to homophobic rectal wipes. Uneasy with his own hankering after boys. Son of a right-wing batterer.

Jess froze. "What did you say?"

I gulped. "I… er…"

"Because if you said what I think you said…"

"Um… well…"

"I'm not sure that's a place we want to go…"

I felt my gay pride ire rising. "Why not?"

"Well. Because. We can't… you know… be… you know… in anything. Like that kind of thing."

"Ah. The love that dares not speak its name."

"Huh?"

"Nothing. It's from a poem by Alfred Douglas. A line used at Oscar Wilde's gross indecency trial."

"Who's he?"

"A writer. Playwright. Dead."

"He was a 'mophobe?"

"No. Just a fag. Punished for it, too."

"Really?"

"Yeah. Jess. Back to us, please."

"Us. Yeah, us." He sat up.

I did too. "And love."

"Yeah. About that." Jess looked thoroughly uncomfortable. And still beautiful. "I dunno if I'm ready for that. You know."

"Me neither, Jess. Who's ever ready? Is that how it happens? You're somehow ready. Then bang! You're in love? I doubt it.

"Look, I'm not apologizing for saying it. But I'm not asking for commitment here, either. I'm going away, after all, in the not-to-distant future. To dance."

"Exactly."

"Exactly what?"

"Exactly why we should avoid the subject."

"Ok. Then what do you feel? For me, I mean. If not love, anything?"

"Yeah."

"Ok. What then?"

Jess sighed. "I… mean I already told you. I like you as more than a friend."

"Fine."

"You're pissed off."

"No. Just disappointed."

"Aw. Come on. Here we are. Together. Nowhere else I wanna be right now. You?"

I looked at him. "No. Nowhere else."

"Let me make it up to you…"

"TOUCHDOWN!!! Did you see that, Ian???" Jess, on his feet and whooping, jolted me back to the game. At that same instant, Mom popped in with snacks and drinks for 'us boys.' She positively beamed on her way out the door.

"Your mom's cool."

"Yeah. Suzette Trudeau." I knew this was her way of keeping a little eye on the two of us. "Coolest mom on the block."

Jess leaned in to me. "So whaddya think, Ian? Would she be cool with us making out here in the living room?"

"Jess. Eeew. Gross."

He snorted. "Just joshin' ya, man!"

In an effort to continue my sports education—ok, so that was just my excuse—Tilly and I began to frequent Jess's hockey games at the arena. At least, thanks to my uncle, I know a little about hockey. Enough to do the wave with the other hockey fans when Jess's team pulled into the lead. Enough to holler in pride and joy when Jess, a forward, scored the winning goal against the visiting team. And enough to beat it after he nodded at me on the way past our seats near the home team bench on his way to the dressing room.

Tilly and I went for pizza afterwards.

"It's such crap, Tilly." I slurped my Coke glumly.

"Uh huh."

"Like, it's not as if we'd make out in public or anything. Neither of us is like that."

"Me either."

I accepted another slice of pizza. Spicy Thai chicken. Our favourite. "But like now… we can't… Jess and I can't just, you know… go for pizza."

"I guess not."

"Well, we can't."

"Well, *you* would. He's too much of a coward."

I looked out our booth across at Todd Ruzicka making the moves on Mindy Schwanke. Todd, who for sure was still seeing Brigit Lowe because we'd just been grossed out by the two of them actively snogging at the hockey game less than one hour ago. Would Todd's little indiscretion with Mindy get back to Brigit,

I wondered. Probably not. Nothing wrong with a little hetero hootch any which where, is there?

I sighed. "Yeah. Maybe. I would be fine having pizza in public, even right here in our little wannabe city. Then again, maybe not. I value my life."

"Well, think of it this way. If you were at this moment out with Jess, you'd be missing this very excellent opportunity to dine with an intelligent Métis hottie who is also a dazzling conversationalist!"

I laughed. "Yeah. No kidding. And you, likewise, would be missing out on stuffing your face across from an absolutely drop dead gorgeous gay danseur!"

"You better believe it!"

We toasted with our Cokes and laughed again. Todd Ruzicka swung around on his thick red neck to give us a sneer.

I stifled my impulse to ask how Brigit was doing. Instead, we just ignored him. And I got to live another night.

But I couldn't ignore the reality that Easter was only a few weeks away. Which meant that my dance rehearsals intensified and I saw Jess less often and pined for him even more.

He stopped me after physics one chilly afternoon.

"What gives?" Jess whispered.

I tried to explain. "I'm busy."

"Is this because of that conversation we had?"

"No."

"Are you sure?"

"Yes, I'm sure!"

Then it happened. McDade and Greene came up behind Jess. He saw my eyes widen, probably in horror, and turned around.

"Hey, guys!" His voice had a nervous edge.

"S'up, Campeau? Little danceboy bugging ya?" McDade sniffed. Greene glared at me.

"Naw."

"'Cause we could teach him a few new steps, eh?"

"No. Trudeau's my physics tutor."

"Yeah?" McDade looked suspicious.

Jess had completely recovered his hetero façade. "Yeah. My old man threatened to pull me off the team if my grades don't improve."

I held my breath. Which team, I wondered. Jess is on so many. Even though he really plays for my team.

McDade sniffed again. "Ok. Well, don't catch anything, Campeau." And he and Greene yukked it up off down the hall in the direction of the cafeteria.

"I'll be over tonight… for homework help." Jess grinned and backed away from me.

That little episode was, I figured, the closest he would ever come to a public admission.

He came that night as promised. And stayed long after Mom finally went to bed.

Jess told me his dad was due home on leave for spring break. We would need to see each other even more secretly, when we could. Between my school, work, rehearsal, preparation for National Ballet School and his practices and smouldering volcanic father.

More stolen moments.

FIFTEEN
Bad Romance

Along with chocolate bunnies and eggs—a relationship I never could quite fathom, I guess kind of like some straight people don't get gay marriage—Easter marks the all-important spring dance program at our dance academy. It is the major performance of the year. And it sends Madame into a tizzy.

This big promotional event requires that sponsors and board members and donors be invited. And not just invited. Impressed. So we must all work very hard all year and especially all spring to be ready in order to impress the dignitaries. Oh yes, and our parents.

But most of all, most importantly of all, crucial to our very survival, we must all work very, very hard to impress Madame. Or else.

Her neatly coifed hair becomes frazzled. Her makeup during later rehearsals is frightening. She smokes incessantly and often forgets her lit cigarettes in various ashtrays. Outside the building. Inside her rat's nest of a firetrap office. She curses in Russian. Usually at either or both Leonora and me. Barks out orders. Makes diva demands for coffee. Aspirin. Screams about the tempo of the music. Wipes the floor with her assistant choreographer.

Personally, at this time of year, I think Madame roams the night skies as a vampire.

Well, the woman looks like she hasn't truly slept in a hundred years by the evening of dress rehearsal.

And also by the evening of dress rehearsal she usually has someone in tears. This year it was Leonora. I was trying to comfort her in the hallway near the washrooms when Jess Campeau walked by.

"Hey."

"H-hey." I was stunned. Jess had told me that he could not, would not come to the dance performance. It was just too risky. With his father home and all.

"I never said anything about dress rehearsal." And he disappeared into the men's can.

I calmed Leonora enough to send her back to the dressing room. Then pushed open the door of the washroom. Jess was drying his hands.

"I-I don't know what to say."

"Nothin' to say. It was supposed to be a surprise." He dried his hands and turned to me. "But there's no keeping secrets from you, is there Trudeau?"

He gave me a kiss for luck and left the washroom just as another patron walked in.

I beat it backstage and tried to calm my racing pulse. Jess was there to see me dance. I could not, would not let him down.

Dress rehearsal is very much a performance. Only there are fewer people in the audience. You could have fooled me. I felt like I was dancing in a major hall filled to capacity. I was filled to capacity. With nerves and joy and well… love.

But throughout, I remained centred.

With the company I was taut, controlled, confident. In the pas de deux with Leonora, I was passionate, attentive, strong, self-assured. But in my solo piece I was on fire. Appropriate for a fire dancer—a human flame leaping across the floor. My height was terrific, and I never even felt the pain in the ankle that I'd injured slightly in rehearsal. It was a soaring, self-assured masculine performance. I got a standing ovation that night. And every night.

But of course, I wanted most to dazzle my forbidden guest in the third row centre.

We went outside behind the building to be alone for a few moments after Madame—in a much better humour—and the other dancers had showered me with post-show kisses and congratulations.

"Ian. That was… a-amazing!"

I did my best 'aw shucks.'

"I mean it. Wow."

"You've seen me dance before."

"Yeah. But not… not like this."

"Thanks."

"I get it now. You—you're really… great."

I found it hard to meet his eyes. "It meant a lot… so much to me that you came tonight. *All I ever needed,*" I quoted my favourite musical, "*was the music and the mirror and the chance to dance for you.*"

"That's from *A Chorus Line.*" He grinned sheepishly at my utter shock. "I rented it and watched it on the sly a few weeks back. Before my dad came home. Guess I figured I made you watch TSN. Thought I needed a tutorial before your big show."

"Why Jess Campeau! I declare! You are a bona fide homosexual boy, after all."

We laughed and he hugged me. And for those precious few seconds, everything, everything was right in the world.

After the third and final performance Sunday night, after Madame was filled with—there's no other word for it—glee, after Mom and Gramma and Grampa and Tilly and I had calmed down and they'd gone home and I'd tucked myself into bed, I sank into a deep, exhausted dance-sore sleep.

I dreamed I heard a banging on the door. A bogeyman late in the night.

But it was no bogeyman. And it was no dream.

Mom came to my bedroom door. "Ian. It's Jess. You'd better get up."

I did and I threw on some sweatpants and limped into the living room. There was Jess sitting and shivering on our sofa, a towel around his shoulders. He was soaking from the rain. His left eye was a deep purple. One nostril had blood caked around it.

"What the hell? Your dad?"

He nodded.

"Jesus, Jess."

I heard the kettle whistling in the kitchen.

"What happened?"

"He f-found… a program from your show. In my room. And assumed the worst."

I buried my face in my hands. The program from a ballet would likely confirm his worst suspicions about his deviant son. "Shit. Jess. You shouldn't even have picked one up. Why did you keep it?"

"To have something to remember. Seemed so harmless at the time." He shifted position on the couch and winced at a pain in his side. "Anyway, I tried to tell him it was nothing. That me and the guys were crashing the show… but he hit me. And hit me. And hit me."

"My mom tried to stop him. But he threw her into the wall and she fell to the floor. She just sat there. Crying. I went over to her, helped her up. I wanted to—to fucking waste him then, but…I didn't. I couldn't. I'm that much of a- a- l-loser."

"Aw, Jess…"

"Something about my mother's voice, begging me not to do anything. I just can't let her down. She's always so flippin' afraid he'll leave us. That we'll be nothing without the old man. I just wish…"

"What, Jess?"

"I just wish—I'd never been born, you know?"

"Shit. Don't say that."

"It's true. Everyone would be better off."

"Not true, Jess. It's not."

His big shoulders shook. I waited, my chest tight and hurting, for him. Finally, he paused and blew his nose.

"Then what happened?"

He shrugged. "And then I broke away and ran out of the house. I just ran and ran in the rain. I didn't know where else to go. So I… so I came here."

"And that's just fine," Mom announced as she brought in a steaming mug of tea. "You're welcome here, Jess."

I loved my mother more than I ever had at that moment.

"Drink this," she handed him the mug. "Then get yourself into the shower and Jess will find you something dry to wear."

He took a few slurps while Mom gathered more towels and got the hot water started in the shower.

I sat with him and felt utterly helpless. "Where does it hurt?"

He half-laughed. "Where doesn't it?"

"Anything broken?"

"Don't think so."

"Your nose?"

"Just bloodied. Nothing worse than what's been done to it in hockey."

"What an asshole!"

"He's my dad. He's got a right."

"Not to hit you! Beat up his own son!"

"No. Not that."

"Then what right has he got, for god's sake?"

"To expect a straight son."

Jess showered and changed. We pumped him full of Advil and tea. Made him put an icepack on his eye. Mom prepped a bed for him on the sofa and then turned in.

I sat on the floor beside my wounded houseguest. Just to be there for him as he fell asleep.

"Thanks, Ian." His voice was very drowsy and his eyes were closed.

"For what?"

"Letting me crash here."

"Of course…" I was going to say that he'd do the same for me, but we both knew that wasn't true.

"I'm still glad, you know. That I saw you dance. It was worth it."

I shook my head, but Jess's eyes were shut. Getting beat up for watching me dance. It was enough to make you weep. I almost started bawling right then and there.

The house was very quiet but for the tapping of the sleet-rain on the eaves outside. I could hear Jess's breath, even and deep. I got up to go back to my room. He caught my hand, held it in a club handshake.

"I love you. Ian."

He left after breakfast. Despite my mother's and my protests. She offered to go with him. Talk to his dad.

But Jess would have none of it.

I wandered through the week in a daze. Filled with dread and hope.

He came back to school on Thursday. I hadn't heard from him. Not even a text. And I didn't dare call him, Facebook or email him. His father had access to the computer; the house phones had call display.

Jess saw me in the hall. Looked at me. Looked quickly away. And said nothing. Not a word. Didn't talk to me all day. Not even in physics. Not after school. He didn't reply to my texts and he wouldn't answer his cell or his land phone when finally, with my stomach in my mouth, I called. No one picked up. Not even the answering machine. No exchange on Friday at school either. I sent him notes that went unanswered. I even tried to corner him in an all but deserted hallway, but he just walked around me.

By Saturday night, I was a mess. An absolute snotty, blubbering, inconsolable mess.

"It's his dad, Ian. His dad must have made a threat." Tilly's voice was soothing over the phone. "Jess must be terrified."

I tried to console myself. Tried not to cry. Tried to understand without understanding. Put it in some kind of perspective. But each day got progressively worse. And each night more nightmarish.

Why didn't he call? Confide in me? Why didn't he trust me?

Jesus! I knew what to do to help. We could get him and his mom some kind of assistance. My mother and I volunteer at the shelter, after all.

His silence was killing me. And as I'd recently learned, I'm not very good at silence. I didn't know how to read it except as rejection.

That's exactly what I felt. Rejected. Powerless.

I felt angry, too. At ending up in this place. This nowhere land. I was pissed at Jess's parents. Pissed at Jess.

Couldn't he recognize that I was in this along with him? That I might be suffering, too?

I guessed he had his own solutions. Didn't need me. Didn't want me.

And that made me feel even worse.

Unnecessary. Forgettable.

So we'd come this far, but no further. None of Jess's words or actions had really meant anything.

Jess Campeau didn't love me.

Never had.

Never would.

"We're going shopping," Tilly announced on a Thursday after school two weeks later.

"What?"

"For my grad dress. That will cheer you up."

I sighed. Grad was the furthest thing from my mind. My only thoughts were…

"Look, Ian. You have got to stop obsessing about him or you will make yourself sick. You've already lost weight."

It was true. I had. I was looking positively gaunt after two weeks of the silent treatment from Jess. And my dancing was definitely suffering because of it.

"Fine. Okay. Shopping."

"And you're coming to my soccer game on the weekend. I know for a fact that it doesn't conflict with your rehearsals because I checked with your mom."

"You did?"

"I did. And she's worried about you, too."

"Great." Just what I needed. The third degree from my mother.

"So no word yet from Jess?"

"No, Mom." I shovelled a forkful of tuna casserole into my mouth.

She waited while I chewed. Took a sip of her tea. Then continued. "Tilly says you've been very upset. Have you?"

"I guess."

"Why didn't you come to me?"

"What and have you rock me to sleep? Call Jess up and confront him? Or worse, go over to his parents' place and spill the beans about his gaydom?" I held back tears. Of grief and anger. "What exactly can you do, Mom? You can't fight this battle for me. And besides it's really none of your business!"

She spoke softly into her mug of Earl Grey. "I could be there for you, son."

I got up and left the table, silently cursing Tilly.

But I went to her soccer game. Cheered her on. Sat with the parents of the team players in the bleachers of the soccer field. No one harassed me. It all felt well... better.

Until I saw them.

Jess Campeau and Brittany Westlock. Entwined. At the south end of the bleachers. Brittany the apple-cheeked cheerleader. Long legs. Wheat blonde hair. Ample breasts. The perfect camouflage for a gay-boy-playing-straight.

So this was what he'd been doing while I'd been tormented for the past seventeen rotten days and miserable nights. While he was ignoring me, he was busy pretending. Playing hetero. Wiping me out of his life. Denying that there was ever a "we." After I'd comforted him in his hour of need, the coward, this was his response.

I made some excuse to Tilly that I had to beat it after the game. Tried to slip away unseen. But it wasn't a very big crowd. After all, girls' soccer isn't the draw of guys' hockey or football. Jess and Brittany—deliberately or accidentally—caught up with me.

"Hey, Trudeau!"

I froze. Kept my back to him.

"Trudeau! Hey! Don't be such a snob."

Still I refused to look at him.

"Trudeau!"

I turned around very slowly. "My name's Ian!"

"Yeah. I know. Ian. I'd like you to meet Brittany."

What did he expect, the jerkoff? That we'd shake hands and all go out for sodas afterwards? Pretend that I was fine with all of this? It was tantamount to betrayal, as far as I was concerned.

"You're the dancer, right?" Brittany cooed.

"Yes. That's right." I wanted to punch out her Chiclet teeth, slap her Cover Girl face. Instead, I turned to go.

"Ian! I'll call you later, okay? This weekend. About that physics homework."

"Don't bother. I'll be busy." For the rest of my life, I wanted to add.

"We're going shopping for my grad dress!" Tilly, my ever-faithful, ever-watchful guardian angel, slipped her arm through mine protectively. She walked me away. Safely away. And whispered all the right consoling why-we-hatey-hatey-hatey-Jess-Campeau comments in my burning ears.

Behind us I heard Brittany snicker. "Boy, he's pretty pissy. Must be jealous or something."

That night I Facebooked him. Even though it was understood that his computer was not secure from his father. I couldn't have cared less. I knew I had something that needed saying. Two words. On his wall.

BASTARD PRICK!!!

Tilly posted a comment moments later: 👍 Tilly likes this!

SIXTEEN
Crying Shame

"**M**aybe this isn't the best way to go about it…"

Tilly, her mom, younger brother and sister and I had been traversing Franken-mall for hours, on a seemingly pointless mission.

To seek out and find the perfect grad dress. For Tilly. Not me.

Actually, the shopping was also for me. A diversion. So I would stop compulsively thinking about that waste of skin. So that I could erase him from my memory. Delete Janus-faced Jess from my files. Hit 'Control Alt Delete' on that Campeau con. Scratch out his beautiful face from all the photos in my head. Lock up the liar back in the closet with his other skeletons. Erase him from my Favourites. Toss him like salad from my thoughts.

So far it was working really well for me.

So far, we'd found nothing resembling an appropriate grad dress for Tilly. Nyet. Nada. Nein. Nothing.

Well, not within our price range, anyway.

And so far I wasn't sure which I least preferred: the personal hell of my disastrous love life and bleeding broken heart. Or the hell of this daylong sojourn at the ugliest and biggest church of consumer worship. The monster mall. With Tilly's family in tow.

All the while Percy talked incessantly about the rides. Which ones he'd puked on. Which ones people had died on. Meanwhile, Régine whined about why she didn't get to have a new dress, too. She had very little pleasant to say to anyone. About anything. Everything. She was fourteen and therefore everything sucked. That girl's hair. That shop clerk's fake smile. That mannequin's left eye.

By three pm, I was considering homocide.

Mrs. Monpetit plodded steadfastly on. Unbothered by her sniping offspring. Even Tilly was tiresome.

"I'm never going to find anything."

"Yes, you will."

"Not within our price range."

"Yes, you will. Your kokum sent us some extra money."

"She did. Wow. That's nice." Tilly was quiet for a moment. I knew her grandparents had very little extra cash to spare. "But still. Grad dresses cost hundreds and hundreds. Thousands even. We'll never find anything we can afford."

"Yes, we will."

Mrs. Monpetit was so certain. I wanted to believe her. But even my faith was becoming shaky. After five hours with her three ill-tempered children.

And then we found the store. La Fabrique. Very chi chi and trendy and ooh la la. Percy and Régine gagged and bolted to the nearby arcade. We three meandered around the store, admiring the garments while grooving to the European dance tunes. There was a second floor to the boutique. Tilly and I climbed the stairs. And gasped together when we saw it. Lemon chiffon. Matching shoes and handbag.

Mrs. Monpetit glanced at the price tag and handed the dress to her eldest. Tilly darted into the change room. Then I looked at the price and gulped. Mrs. M. was looking at the cost of the shoes and handbag, too.

She kept her face very still. She opened her purse. Unzipped a compartment. Brought out a wad of bills, many of them weathered and tattered. She began counting. I began sweating. Next she fished out her change purse. Poured its contents into her palm. A tiny furrow of her eyebrow. I reached into my jeans pocket and found my wallet. Dug around in my pocket again for change. Handed her $11.76.

She nodded and took the money. "We've got enough for the dress and the bag." Gave me back twenty-six cents. "Keep the change, Ian." We chuckled.

And Tilly emerged.

Honestly, she could have perched atop my Gramma's lemon chiffon cake—she was that beautiful.

I really did set aside all thoughts of Jess.

I watched Tilly pose in front of the three-way mirror. "If I was straight..." She laughed and so did I. Then all three of us were hamming it up in front of our reflections. I tried not to notice the woman salesclerk noticing us.

Just as Tilly went to change, Percy and Régine burst in and up the stairs.

"Ma, can we get some French fries?"

Mrs. M. shooed them off. I saw Percy draw his hands through some velvet skirts as he left. This time I couldn't ignore the salesclerk first grimace at Percy, then notice Mrs. M. opening the little lemon clutch purse.

"Is there anything I can help you with?" Her crisp voice jolted us from our pleasant thoughts. She planted herself very near the purse display and Tilly's mother. And finally, finally I saw. The unbearable whiteness of her little teeth and her translucent veiny skin told me all I needed to know about her. Just as she was looking keenly at Mrs. M's skin and making all sorts of stupid asinine assumptions.

"Yes," Mrs. Monpetit spoke calmly, putting the clutch back on the display holder, but not meeting the white woman's eyes. "We'll be taking the matching shoes along with the dress."

"Not the clutch, then."

Tilly and her mom never looked once into those cold eyes throughout the transaction. I was inwardly seething as Mrs. M. counted out the crumpled bills and the mittfuls of change for the exact cost of the dress and shoes plus sales tax. Never once did that awful clerk smile. She looked like she didn't want to touch the money. As if it were dirty. But she took it anyway. They always do.

I wanted to tell her off before we left, but Tilly whispered, "Please no, Ian. Don't."

And I listened. Sanctimonious me. I didn't open my megaphone mouth. But I sure wanted to.

We left the store together, our ears burning. Mine in rage, but Tilly's and her mom's with something else. We found Percy and Régine. Then we found exit 112 of about 30,000. And we found the car in the hideous and maddened parking lot.

Tilly watched her siblings pile into the vehicle. "Too bad about the purse. I'd have liked to complete the outfit." She sighed. "Oh, well. The shoes are sweet. Now I have to learn to walk in them so I don't trip and fall on my face."

Finally, I found my voice. "How often does that kinda stuff happen?"

"That I actually want to buy a pair of pumps? Never. I'm a soccer cleats girl."

"Come on, Tillster. You know what I mean. That stuff with the salesclerk."

Tilly shrugged. "A lot, I guess. To my mom. My brother. My sister and me? Our skin is lighter, so we hardly ever get harassed." We slid into the back seat with Régine and buckled up. "Unless we're with them." She nodded in the direction of her mom adjusting the radio tuning and then at Percy, in the passenger seat.

The nasal twang of some country singer masked our words.

"That's revolting, Tilly. It really is. I can't stand how that witch -with-a-b treated her and you. That racism shit. It starts small. But it mushrooms. Turns into bloodiness. Or worse, wars. Why didn't you say anything? Why couldn't I?"

"Well, it's not really your problem, Ian."

"Yes, it is, Tilly. I mean, isn't it? All our problem? Everyone's?"

Tilly slipped her arm through mine and snuggled close. Her free arm held her precious package. "You're a great friend, Ian. You really are."

"Then I should have said something in your defence, Tilly."

"No, I should have said something. In my own defence."

Was she afraid of embarrassing her mother? Was she too shy? "Why didn't you, Till?"

"I will, Ian. Someday. I will."

SEVENTEEN
What a Fool Believes

I was still fuming about that racist excuse for a salesclerk that same night, imagining smart, blistering retorts instead of doing my social studies homework, when the phone rang.

"Hello?"

"Hi, Ian. It's Jess."

I hung up. Simultaneously congratulating myself for my bravery and berating myself for my immaturity.

He called back within a minute.

"Hey, Ian. Look, don't hang up okay? I'm at a payphone and this is the last of my change. Just hear me out."

I told myself, 'Ian, you are too dumb for words,' but aloud I said, "Ok. Fine. I'm listening."

"H-how are you?"

"Gee, Jess. I'm just dandy. Absofrickinlutely fabulous. How are you? Sure nice chatting with you. Ba bye now."

"Wait! Ian! Wait! I'm sorry. I know you… you must feel like… like…"

"Like crap? Camel dung? Cow pie? Fag feces? Yep. All of that and so much more."

"Ian. You gotta believe me. I feel the same. I do. Only. I had to do it. Pull away. Give us space.

"When I got home the morning after I stayed at your place, my dad was already working on changing the locks on the doors. My mom had been up crying most of the night. I guess they'd had more words. Over me."

There was a long pause.

"She made me promise, Ian. Promise not to do anything. You know. To upset Dad. For her sake, Ian. She said she couldn't live with the tension between us. Or with me kicked out of the house. She didn't know what she'd do if she lost me. I mean if you could have seen her… so scared. Small. Helpless even.

"I don't know how else to explain it. I can't expect my mom to stand up to my dad. She's terrified of him. We're all terrified of what he'd be capable of if we fought back. Shit. Even our cocker spaniel is scared of him when he blows.

"So I promised. To behave. However she wanted. To be the good straight son.

"I went up to dad and I told him that the guys and I had only been having a little fun at the expense of the dance school. Heckling the dancers. And I told him I was seeing Brittany. He knew I was already going to grad with her. So I convinced him that she had been hitting on me all term—which was true—and I was going to bring her for supper the next Sunday.

"He bought it. Apologized for socking me. Gave me a key to the new lock. And I brought her over. The whole incident blew over as if Dad forgot it. And me and Britt started up, you know, as an official couple. But I don't feel anything for her, Ian. Not like I feel for you. But I can't… I can't… change. I'm s-sorry."

His voice broke up on the other end of the line. I didn't trust my own to say much except "I'm sorry, too."

I could hear Jess blow his nose. "Y-you must hate me."

"No, Jess. That's not true." I thought to myself, there's enough hate in your life. You don't need anymore. "I feel pretty helpless, is all, being shut out like that."

"I really want to see you, Ian..."

"You do?"

"Maybe when my dad leaves again..."

What could I say? He still liked me? Wanted to see me? My abandoned mine of a heart cracked open, ever so slightly, to allow in a beam of light. "What about Brittany? She has feelings for you."

"Jesus, Ian. I don't know what to do about that. I'm kinda working this out as I go. Just stay with me here. See me again. When we can."

"O-okay."

"It's not okay. But it has to be for now."

"You could have told me all this sooner, Jess. I've been kind of going crazy, you know."

"I'm sorry."

"I thought you didn't... you know... give a rat's ass about me."

"That's not true, Ian, I swear."

"I've been a mess, my life pretty much a cesspool. You could've... we could've found a way to communicate. Somehow."

"That's why I'm calling. I – I wanted to talk to you. Thought about calling a ton of times. Then I talked myself out of it. Because I thought you'd be ashamed of me."

"What?" but inwardly I groaned. I knew what was coming.

"Because you... you would have stood up to your old man. Fought back probably. Done the right thing."

Would I? I didn't have Frankenstein for a father. I don't have a father. Period. What would I do? People assume stuff. Like about what a person would really do. Under similar circumstances. I'd probably have run away—my usual life-saving strategy. But to Jess and others I'd set myself up as some kind of champion of causes, some false saviour-figure. Like I did with Tilly earlier that day. Or when I told on Kato over Régine being harassed. Or when I participated over-zealously in things like Amnesty letter-writing day through our SPAM school club. Or when I think I know every-bloody-thing in social studies class, just like Erika the Goth said. I must give off the stench of righteousness.

Gag.

What a joke. Truth is I'm just a gay boy luckily born into the right family in the right country in the right century.

When you get right down to it, what would I do in Jess's shoes? What would I have done if my mom had begged me to make such a promise? Would I be going steady with Tilly? Bet your ass, I would.

"You know, Jess. You have to do what you have to do. I just hope one day it's better for you. I wish I could make it better for you." I caught myself. No more Mr. Messiah. "But I can't. Because I'm still a minor. And so are you. And we're kind of trapped as minor minorities. In this predicament. You way worse than me."

"Yeah. I guess you're right there…"

"I'm not always right, Jess."

"Pretty much."

I felt guilty hearing the admiration in his voice. I'd been secretly calling Jess Campeau every unflattering name I could think of for the past few weeks. Barely thinking of what could have driven him to cut me out of his life. Really only thinking of my own misery. "One day soon you'll be a legal adult. You'll have more options."

"Yeah, one day." There was silence on the other line. "Ian," he said quietly. "D-do you forgive me?"

"Yeah." I did. His was an impossible situation. He was so trapped. And I'd played my part in keeping us apart. I saw that now. "Try not to be such an asshole next time." And I'll try, too, I told myself.

Jess half-chuckled. "I'll try. But it runs in the family."

So break the pattern, I thought to myself. But I kept my big opinionated trap shut. Ian the grand moralizer. Ian with all the easy answers. Suddenly, I was pretty sick of myself and what my smugness had cost me.

"I'll see you around, Ian."

I didn't want him to hang up. Sever this re-connection. "When?"

He sounded sad. "Dunno."

I took a deep breath. "What are you doing right now?"

"Talking to you. At a 7-11 payphone. At the stripmall near your place."

"Where do your parents think you are?"

"Out for the night. With Brittany."

"Come over, Jess."

"Really?"

I never meant anything more in my life. "Pretty much. Yeah."

So he came over. And I let Jess Campeau in. Again.

EIGHTEEN
Mamma Mia

Yes, colour me stupid. Slag my hypocritical rainbow ass. I became—again—a willing accomplice to the dirty little secret that was Jess's entire life.

Only this time it was even worse. I surrendered any control. We played exclusively by Jess's rules. And they were harsh. Because they had to be. Neither of us wanted his father to catch any whiff of the fact his son was gay. The price was too high. So this time there was no physics homework tutoring. No café tête-à-têtes. No workouts. No daylight contact whatsoever.

It felt repulsive.

Really I was only a ladder rung up from one of Whitleigh's English teachers, Mrs. Jacob. Reliable tongues wagged rumours about her secret liaisons with students in darkened parking lots or deserted classrooms, long after official school hours.

And I felt as dirty as Ms. Sainte and Mr. Hardy, two phys ed teachers, who were quietly "disappeared" from our school after a student discovered them doing the nasty on the mats—sans lights—in a gym storage room.

As creepy as Mr. Robinson, the neighbour on our street who watches *every*day, in his bathrobe, from his front picture window as the little kids come home from school.

Because we crept around, me and Jess. Like creatures of the night. Behind closed doors. After hours. In the shadows. The middle of the night. I felt like I was dating a vampire. Thought about re-christening myself: Sookie Stackhouse II.

It was awful. But it was better than nothing. Which was what I had from him during the day. Daytimes were the worst.

Because I'd see him. And I wasn't allowed to. And I saw all too much of Jess Campeau in the daylight.

Everywhere.

In the line-up for the cafeteria. Coming out of the guys' can. Hand in hand with Brittany in the halls. Two seats over every day in physics. Playing field hockey in the sports field. Sharing some joke with McDade and Greene at the water fountain.

I tried avoiding him. Hanging out almost exclusively in the library. But Jess somehow found his way in there, too. Would brush by me as I sat at the computer. It was torture.

I considered cutting physics class, but it was my senior year and I HAD to keep my grades up.

He wasn't mean or unpleasant. Said hi sometimes. Nodded at me.

And there was still no graffiti on my locker.

I just felt invisible. Invisible Ian. Who was slowly dying inside.

It's a funny thing about love.

Starts off pretty wonderfully with your stomach doing somersaults for joy. You look forward to seeing the person wherever and however often you can. Find excuses for calling and talking.

Sending texts. Notes. Emails. You can't get enough of each other. Or you think you'll die. You have trouble concentrating. Every little thing—your hair, what you wear, what you say, how you eat—is considered in the light of the other. What will the person think of this? of that? of you? You kind of live for the person. Give it all up for the person. Get swept up in the idea that the person you love is perfect. Or nearly so.

Then when it comes crashing down and circumstances change for the worse, you still live in the hope of seeing the person. But when you do, your chest gets all constricted. And there's a dull thud in your skull. You still have trouble concentrating. And still every little thing is considered in terms of how the person will see you, if your paths should cross. As they inevitably do. You live to see him. And it kills you when you do.

Because now, every time he enters your line of vision, there's a curious pain that feels like a small rodent is continually eating away at your heart.

Despite how I felt, I had to keep going to school. Keep up my grades. Maintain my fitness and flexibility. All for the National Ballet School.

It had somehow lost its lustre. My dream had soured in the aftermath of meeting Jess and losing Jess and then my nocturnal and infrequent meetings with Jess. I willed myself through the days. Tried not to wonder if tonight was a night I'd see him. Willed myself to look forward to the summer. To graduation. To the second stage audition and four weeks in Toronto.

In the evenings I tried not to obsess about him. About us. Tried not to wait for the payphone call that most often didn't come. He didn't dare use his cell to call or text me, so I felt chained to our land phone. I felt chained, period. Like that old Aretha Franklin song: "Chain of Fools."

Torn up about everything—the relationship, the non-relationship, Jess's home life, all the pretense—my body and my stomach hurt most of the time. I was having a tough time eating. Thinking. Caring about much beyond Jess.

Dance was what held me together. Barely. I went to the studio as often as possible, whenever it was open. To grieve. To dance. I pushed myself. As though to make my muscles ache would somehow lessen my heartache.

Madame often watched me. Stood with pursed lips at the studio door. Said nothing except to give the occasional direction.

My mother would frown when I came home late from the studio, but she, too, held her tongue about Jess. She would rub my calves with liniment and chat about mundane things. A family barbecue Gramma and Grampa were planning for the summer. And grad.

The days were gearing up toward the grand affair that marked the supposed end of adolescence and beginning of adulthood. Our collective rite de passage. Graduation. I really had no interest in attending. However, my parent and grandparents had other plans. Plus there was the matter of the brand new suit hanging in my closet. My grandparents' Christmas present. Back when I gave a sweet shit about being part of the graduating class.

And to top it all off, one frosty, supposedly spring day, Erika, Queen of the Night, cornered me just outside the social studies classroom door. I pressed myself against the doorframe and silently wished for a crucifix.

"Trudeau. Know what a flashmob dance is?"

I eyed her suspiciously. Was this a trick question? Or was she looking to disembowel me with her scathing criticism again? "Like the impromptu dances at Central Station in New York?"

She nodded, and I fleetingly also wished I'd worn a garlic bulb necklace that morning.

"Duh."

"That's what I want to do. For grad. Instead of stupid bake sales and bottle drives. I want to do something memorable and fun. A public, spontaneous dance. And I want you," she actually poked me with her black fingernail, "to help."

Memorable and fun? Goth girl? Dancing? Previously I thought her only idea of fun might be dancing on graves. A danse macabre. What did I know? Her nearness was making me nervous. "Ummm... not really my area of expertise..."

Erika fixed me in that withering morbid stare of hers. I felt my flesh crawl.

"But I-I- could give it my best shot. I guess."

"Good answer. Look, my dad is manager of the mall. I've got the local Rogers company to sponsor the event, long as we can get some kids using their phones to advertise the Rogers network."

I must have nodded, because I swear she began to get excited. Well, as excited as the living dead ever get.

"We'll bring in more bucks from one sponsorship than a hundred bake sales. I'm gonna set the time and the public space up —probably the food court. I'll talk to the Whitleigh videography club and get them to film it. It'll be a riot."

"Yeah. A riot."

"The best thing, the most interesting thing a graduating class has ever done. Sure beats the asinine 'pitch and dump.'"

She was, of course, referring to the annual dunk tank where every grad had an opportunity to dump a teacher or two into a swimming pool, with a carefully aimed softball. That was fun maybe a century ago. Fewer and fewer teachers were willing to suffer the humiliation or the chilly spring temperatures just to raise a few dollars for the graduating class. Last year's event was a big bust. Quite literally. When the school councellor and Life Management teacher, Mrs. Burbank's big left titty fell out of her swimming suit on impact with the water. You can still find it on YouTube, if you look hard enough.

"You'll be responsible for the music and the moves, Trudeau. Think ABBA. Think Lady Gaga. Think K-OS. Well, I trust your instincts."

This was news to me. I was dazed and confused that Erika was even talking to me, given that not long ago she had been poised to rip my throat out. And however did she know about ABBA and Gaga and K-OS? I thought she fed on a steady diet of bands like Slipknot and Marilyn Manson.

"Um- well, Erika, there's just one thing... I-I- don't get it. I really thought that you... you know, had a hate on me."

"Get over yourself. I don't *hate* you Trudeau. I just think you wank off too much. Sometimes. In this instance..." she smiled, and fascinated, I couldn't stop staring at her canines—they looked like they'd been filed to points. "Trudeau, especially in this instance, I believe you can be most helpful."

"Ah- okay. I guess."

"Create altogether about a four-minute dance sequence. I'll help with recruitment. We'll post your choreography on YouTube."

"Great." I envisioned maybe three hits: Tilly's, mine, and Erika's.

"And one other thing..." Her grin was broad as a skeleton's. "I really like Michael Jackson's *Thriller*. See if you can work that into the dance, okay?"

Erika liked Michael Jackson? Well, of course there was the ghoul factor of *Thriller*. I could certainly see how that would have Goth appeal. But Erika liked to dance? And now Erika was deigning to ask me to be part of something for grad? And under her hypnotic trance, I found myself agreeing. What was wrong with me? Did I have some kind of death wish?

"Oh, and you'll never guess who's agreed to be my perfect pretty faces promoting Rogers' network with their cellphones…"

"Who?"

"Who else but the prettiest of the pretty people? I appealed to their vanity. Told them this could make them instant YouTube celebs. That worked in a heartbeat! They couldn't resist the lure of the camera and their shot at fame, quelle surprise!"

I felt dizzy all of a sudden. "Don't tell me…"

"None other than the current coolest couple of Whitleigh: Brittany Westlock and Jess Campeau."

Right then, I did a little vomit in my mouth.

NINETEEN
It Goes On and On and On and On

So despite my misgivings—and I had many—I set to work. If only to distract myself from my romantic fixation. First thing was to text Tilly and get her in on this flashmobberie:

R U 4 real, Ian? Of course, I'll dance with you! Coolio!

I'm gonna ask the hiphop dancrs at the studio to help. Can U B there at 3:15, T-ster?

Gr8 idea! C U then.

Next, I recruited three hip hop and jazz dancers to help with some of the snazzier moves. I am, after all, a classically-trained ballet danseur. What I know about hip hop I've learned from watching the hip hop teacher and goofing around with the girls in Saturday jazz classes at the studio sometimes. Best to rely on the experts to get buck to a beat.

Third, I downloaded the songs: ABBA's "Mamma Mia," Lady Gaga's "Poker Face," K-OS's "Crabbuckit," Michael Franti's "Say Hey," Tchaikovsky's "Waltz of the Flowers," Michael Jackson's "Thriller," and finally, my pièce de resistance, Avril Lavigne's "Girlfriend." Okay, well, I only had to download one song. I had all the others on my iPod. Then I cut and edited them together to come up with four fantastic minutes. I was quite proud of my deejay mix.

Tilly and my Solid Gold Hip Hop Hotties loved it! They came over to watch the *Thriller* video about a dozen times until we had

Michael's moves down. Then we reviewed the YouTube flashmob dances, all of them that we could find, and all the music videos of the artists, for groove move ideas. It was the best Friday night I'd had in weeks. We made popcorn and popped and laughed our dance-asses off. As if on cue, my mom even wandered in to join us as we discoed to "Mamma Mia."

Then around 11:30 pm the phone rang. Tilly shot me a look as I went into my bedroom to take the call.

"Hello?" I knew who it was.

"Hey, Ian. Zup?"

"Hey, Jess."

"Wanna hook up? I can slip out in about an hour."

"Um. I'm kinda busy. I've got friends over."

"You do?"

"I *have* got friends, Jess."

"I didn't mean that. It's just...well, it's been quite a while since I saw you."

"Yeah, it has." Mentally, I counted about thirteen days and nights off in my head.

"So."

"So what?"

"When do they leave?"

"Look, I don't know, Jess. We're working on that Rogers video flashmob dance sequence. You know the one starring you and boobilicious Brittany?"

"Oh. Yeah. That."

"So, I can't really kick them out, can I?"

"No, I guess not. But when do you think they'll leave?"

"I have no idea. We're working hard on the choreography." Not really the whole truth and nothing but the truth, but I wanted him to at least consider that I had a life beyond him.

"Who's over?"

"Tilly, Trish, Melanie, Stacey, girls from the dance studio. We're deep into the planning stages of Erika's grad project. And…" I added for emphasis, "we're having fun."

"Oh."

I swallowed hard and forced myself to say the words, "So maybe another time, okay?"

"O-Ok."

The disappointment in his voice was delicious. I know it was mean of me to feel that way. But I'd been at his bloody beck and call for weeks. Playing the waiting game. This night, this one night was mine.

"Talk to you, Jess."

"Hey, Ian? What about tomorrow?"

I paused for effect. "If I'm free. This is pretty important and the group may need to meet again. We'll see."

"I'll call you. Tomorrow night? Around the same time?"

"Maybe."

My heart was thudding faster than the bass from the TV speakers in the other room. I'd rebuked the love of my life. Just like Bridget Jones did. I felt powerful and simultaneously nauseated. I returned, green-gilled, to the girls.

"I blew him off," I said into Tilly's ear.

She just grinned and pulled me back into the dancing fray at the centre of the living room.

We danced until we dropped and made plans to finalize and polish the choreography at the dance studio on Saturday morning.

I got there early and approached Madame, who looked as if she'd had some horrible vodka nightmare.

"Madame," I helped her off with her velvet cloak and hung it up on her coat rack. "I made fresh coffee."

"Da! Da, coffee. Immediately, my Ee-an. Or I will like to die."

I hustled to produce the black elixir and sat down in the chair opposite her desk. "Madame, I have a favour to ask of you."

"What favour of Madame, my prize?" I could tell she was really only paying attention to adding the six packets of sugar to her dark brew.

"I—uh. I'm involved in a school grad fundraiser. We're choreographing a flashmob dance. It's kind of a spontaneous dance that takes place in a public space—in this case the local mall."

"Da. Mall." She took a sip. Ripped open another sugar packet.

I still didn't have her attention, but I sensed her lack of interest might work in my favour.

"I was wondering if we might use the large dance studio for the next week or so. To practise. Whenever it isn't being used."

Madame took another sip, sighed, and leaned back in her chair. "Fine. Fine. Use. Use. Just to keep it clean. Lights out when done. Locking door. You know rules, Ee-an."

"Thank you, Madame." I rose to go.

"My prize. Pleese. My pills." She touched her forehead, and I knew she meant the aspirin. I rummaged through the storage cabinet on the opposite wall and found them. She took the bottle and spilled out four pills she then downed with her coffee. "My darling. My cigarettes." I fished those, too, out of her cape pocket. Handed them to her. She opened the silver cigarette holder and made a selection.

"Do not ever to smoke, Ee-an. Is dirty habit. If you start, I will like to keel you."

"I won't Madame." I smiled and turned to the door.

"And I will also like to keel you," she said drily to my back, "if dance floor is in anyway damaged. By your leetle project." I heard her strike a match.

"Yes, Madame."

The Solid Goldies arrived by ten am and the five of us rehearsed in one of the smaller dance studios. By noon we were ready. I'd invited Erika to see our fancy footwork which was pretty inventive without being too hard for people to learn.

And Erika was fairly impressed for a corpse. "Gee, Trudeau. You outdid yourself." There was actually admiration in her voice.

Goth girl was beginning to grow on me. Kind of like a wart.

She'd brought along her camera and tripod to tape our instructional video. At three pm she'd already posted it on YouTube and started a Facebook invitation to view the site and learn the dance. It was a closed group event, open only to certain invited friends. The date for the flashmob was set. Everyone had a week to learn and rehearse the dance moves. I posted a rehearsal schedule for all six times the large studio was empty.

We would begin rehearsals on Monday.

It was so exciting, I could hardly eat my mom's famous French onion soup. After all the flurry of the day, it was hard to settle down. Especially when I tried to do my homework and read the novel we were working on for English. Finally, I flipped on the tube and watched *SNL*. Then *Conan*. Started up my computer to check the YouTube page. Eighty-eight hits already. Erika was a get 'er done kinda girl. I smiled and watched us mugging and moving on the little screen. The computer clock said 2:23 am.

I pulled on my hoodie and slipped out the back door. Took myself for a walk under the streetlights and wandered over to the 7-11. Checked the payphone for change. There was none. Headed back to Oriole and passed again beneath the streetlamps. Some burb worker bee had finally fixed the usually broken one so I could find my way safely home.

I crawled into bed at 3:40 am. Listened through my earphones to the *Glee* cast sing Journey's "Don't Stop Believing."

But I'd already stopped.

Saturday night had come and gone.

And the phone never rang once.

TWENTY

Flashdance...What a Feeling!

Monday.

I felt ornery. Contrary. I wanted Jess to feel uncomfortable. Because he'd made me feel invisible again. Unimportant. Undone. Un.

So I decided to look at Jess every chance I got. Really look. Turn my head with intent. Every time he passed my way. I deliberately *saw* him. Whether or not he was with Brittany or the boys. Whether in physics or in the halls. I made eye contact. Most often he'd look away. Sometimes he gave me a quizzical glance. I didn't stare. I just made sure he saw me seeing him.

Others noticed, too. I overheard Brittany say as we crossed paths, "I think he has a crush on you, Jess." I smiled to myself. If only she knew.

By midweek, he'd had enough. His phone call woke me late at night.

"What the hell are you tryin' to pull, Ian?"

"Jess. It's after midnight. And a weeknight. You probably woke my mom."

"Answer my question."

I knew what he meant. "I just *see* you, is all. For what you really are. I want to *see* you. And I want you to *see* yourself. And I want you to *see* me. You aren't invisible. Not to me. And I don't want to be invisible to you."

"How many times do I gotta explain? I can't be visible. Or out. I CAN'T!"

"Everything is always on your terms, Jess."

"Look, what do you want from me, Ian? My dad. My dad has a stranglehold on me. On Mom. What don't you get about that?"

"You're a big boy, Jess. Something, sometime has to give."

"Being big's got nothin' to do with it. He's got some kinda power... I can't explain. I always feel like I'm about five years old around him. Like everything could just crumble and fall, if he loses it entirely. You must get that, don't you? You seemed to. Anyways, I- I thought you did. When I told you that personal stuff..."

I sighed. Of course, I did. I was just being stubborn. "I've got every right to pay attention to anyone I want to."

"I'm asking you... not to... not to make it obvious how you feel about me, Ian. Please. For your own good. And mine, too."

"And how do you feel about *me*, Jess?"

"Jesus, Ian..."

"Seriously. Because when you didn't call, I felt like toejam football."

"How do you think I felt? I wanted to. I was dying inside. But I was trapped in the house with my old man who was tossing back the rye and arguing with my Mom. He was gettin' ugly. Drink makes him uglier. There was no way I could leave her alone that night."

"Oh. I didn't know."

"Don't you think I wanted to see you, too? That night? That I want to see you at school? That I want to see you right now?"

"You do?"

"This is the best I've got, Ian. Right now."

So I eased up on the eyeballing. Concentrated on the dancing. Rehearsals for the flashmob were going really well and altogether, we had about fifty dancers in total. Included in this total were Erika Herself (who, I begrudgingly noted, was a good dancer) and Tilly's younger siblings, Régine and Percy, who had some excellent b-girl/b-boy breaker moves. The final countdown was on. At the last rehearsal, Erika took in our consent forms, ensuring that all the confirmed participants gave their or their parents' permission to be filmed and posted and screened. Goth girl was nothing if not thorough.

She, Tilly and I met Friday night at BP to strategize over appies and bevvies. Brittany and Jess joined us an hour later to discuss their positions and movements in the mall and the logistics of the filming. Ironically, after my "I-*see*-you stunt" earlier in the week, in the enclosed space of the restaurant booth, I found it difficult to look at Jess. My cheeks were on fire the entire time. So much for not giving my feelings away.

At 2:15 pm on Saturday, I was window-shopping at the mall with Tilly. We each carried a shopping bag, so as to appear legit. Crowds were pretty good because there was an antique car show featured all weekend. Nothing like antique cars to pull in the sub-urbane lemmings. Plus there were a number of people who knew about the event and wanted to witness our hijinx. I saw members of the videography club wandering about, trying to look unobtrusive, with the school's small video cameras slung over their shoulders. I even saw Mr. Deede, the video club supervisor teacher, pretending

to be a passerby in the mall. And in the Body Shop I caught sight of Brittany and Jess. He lifted his chin in greeting.

Tilly and I meandered over to the food court. There is a big area, framed by six pillars with huge mounted speakers, directly across from the restaurant kiosks and tables. It's where the mall employees sometimes erect a stage for fashion shows or, at Christmas time, set up Santa's sleigh for the big guy and his elves. But that Saturday it was just empty space.

At 2:30 sharp, someone killed the dreadful seventies mall muzak.

The loudspeakers boomed out the opening strains and then "mum mum mum mah." I threw my bag down and leapt to the centre of the bare floor where, solo, I began the side step and arm thrusts, just as we'd practised. Some astonished shoppers stopped, slack-jawed. Tilly threw down her bags and joined me just as Lady Gaga began singing. By the chorus, the entire Solid Gold team of five was strutting its stuff, modelling our best Gaga poker faces. A small crowd was now gathering. Out of the corner of my eye I saw a video camera. I knew there were two others, elsewhere, simultaneously shooting the footage.

The music switched to the tinkling perfect fifths of ABBA's signature hit, and as they heard the beginning strains, a few more "shoppers" abandoned their bags and joined in with our disco moves. By now people were on to us. Many were straining to see, cellphones raised above heads to film the action. A number of faces in the crowds were familiar ones from school, but most were simply strangers, unsuspecting mall patrons, shocked and amazed.

I was grinning my fool head off and so was Tilly. So were the other Solid Gold Hip Hop Hotties.

Now the mood changed as "Waltz of the Flowers" kicked in. We seamlessly found partners and bowed, each to the other. A formal waltz ensued, and again several mall "customers" simply stopped shopping, and effortlessly joined in. It was fantastic! Crowds were beaming and swaying alongside of the dancers.

Romantic turned to funkilicious fun with K–OS's "Crabbuckit." We did our revolution struts with the addition of still more dancers, including Tilly's b–girl sister, Régine. Then we added in some zoot suit groove moves, and for a flourish, Tilly's brother, Percy, joined in with his own breaking moves that sent the audience into a fit of spontaneous applause.

A burst of famously evil laughter from Vincent Price signalled the next shift as we assumed the V–position of the iconic Michael Jackson *Thriller* video. And though we wore street clothes, we were instantly transformed into wild-eyed ghouls and zombies, with me at the point of the triangle, à la Michael. We began the pops and jerks to the bass and rhythm guitar, leading into the hip shakes. When we raised our zombie hands left and then right at the chorus, the audience went mad! I saw Brittany and Jess take their places near one of the pillars, as we'd previously arranged.

A video camera girl quickly swept in to get a close up of their cell phones, flipped open and presumably filming us without a transmission hitch, thanks to Rogers' Wireless network.

"Thriller" ended with a repeat of Vincent Price laughter and a sudden flip into Avril Lavigne's most appropriate-ever refrain: "hey you, I don't like your girlfriend." We mimicked Avril's moves in her video, during the clapping-percussive break. The camera crew came in for some close ups, as we, the five Solid Gold Hotties, moved in on the cool couple of Whitleigh. We cavorted around the two and dragged them with their cellphones into the dance. Caught up in the zeal of the lyrics, it felt great to sing about not liking Jess's girlfriend right to his face, my personal twist on Avril's song.

Finally, the boom beat of Michael Franti's "Say Hey" switched up the dancers into a finale frenzy of love. All fifty were now raising the mall roof. We took up the entire area, and some even spilled into the food court itself. Our energy was infectious. It spread like a virus. I could see mall patrons gettin' their groove on along with us. No one could resist. Toddlers were bouncing. Little kids were shaking what their mamas gave them. Tweens and teens were movin' and groovin'. Adults, shakin' and bakin'. Even some seniors were getting jiggy. Seriously, one old guy was jigging! And everybody, *everybody* was smiling.

It felt incredible. I was the most happy I'd been in my entire life. Those four minutes were pure joy. And I could see it reflected in the faces around me. Tilly's. Even pale Erika's. The Hotties'. My grandparents' I caught a glimpse of in the throng. And Jess Campeau's, too, as he bopped awkwardly along with Brittany. Palpable for four whole minutes, vibrating through that stupid suburban mall: joy. We brought joy to the masses.

So I couldn't help myself. As the final chorus began, as I boogied my butt off, I began to sing my guts out. No one could hear me. But you could easily make out the words, because Franti repeats them so often. Caught up in the exuberance and spirit of Franti's music, I sang "I love you" to Tilly and she gave it right back to me. The Hotties caught on and the refrain rippled through the dancers and into the crowd. Soon everyone gathered was repeating the phrase, and you really could hear us singing above the speakers, it was that loud. That powerful. Jubilant, I repeated, "I love you," as I first I gavotted over to Brittany and then more deliberately towards Jess.

I completely forgot about the cameras recording all of this for posterity.

And just as suddenly as the music began, it stopped. The mall muzak resumed. All the dancers picked up their discarded bags, and melted back into the stream of mall traffic. Tilly and I milled amongst the shoppers, and the whole scene appeared as though nothing had ever happened.

But of course, it had.

TWENTY-ONE

The Sun Will Come Out...Tomorrow

Within an hour, the first YouTube amateur videos were up. Whitleigh's video club would need some time to edit their more professional footage in the school's editing suite before posting. But much of the good fun had been initially captured in the grainy and jerky hand-held cell and iPhone cameras and was already getting hundreds of hits.

Tilly and I celebrated with the Hip Hop Hotties and Erika at my place. My grandparents sprang for pizza. We were in a congratulatory mood and toasted each other incessantly as we watched YouTube like addicts. Colour had even replaced Erika's customary pallor-ridden cheeks, so much that she almost glowed with excitement. The Hotties and I kept high fiving each other.

After one particularly good amateur clip, Tilly turned to me. "Wow, Ian. The choreography is really sick! We pulled the pants down and done spanked that bad boy!!!"

That's when we lost it. The six of us spilled all over the floor laughing until we peed ourselves.

Not that I'm prone to quoting bad lyrics of bad songs or anything, but truly, that Saturday, I had the time of my life.

But it's a virulent cyber world out there. Early Sunday morning the first paparazzi posts appeared. My public profession of love to Jess and dislike of his girlfriend was apparently big juicy news. Amateur filmmakers and pimply-faced blogsters tripped over themselves, Tweeting and Facebooking and YouTubing and blogging and Flickr-ing and GossipRock-ing to the universe at large that Ian Trudeau loved Jess Campeau. Luckily, my cellphone number was known only to family and close friends, so I wasn't also bombarded with ugly text messages.

Did none of these people have lives? Or was it simply that the one known gay kid at Whitleigh Composite High had offered a gross indecency (read: love via a pop song) to the school's most popular jock idol?

And in our perfect suburban paradise, such a thing is expressly verboten.

I had no doubt that most of the perpetrators walked the very halls of Whitleigh. I even had a pretty good idea who some of the authors were, given their lack of imagination and lousy writing skills. These weren't random posts by strangers. Although I did read a few outsiders' comments responding to the various short clips of close-ups of my proclamation to Jess. One calling himself 'Rednecking in Alberta' declared that he had "a solution for ass jockeys like me." Another 'Proud and Rightly Canadian' advised all viewers and readers to "never fear no ass rammer queer" because the "sodomites'" day of doom was a-comin'. Others had helpful advice for me, wherever and whoever I was: "Jesus is your cure."

By noon, I was feeling pretty sick to my stomach. I had to let my mom know what was going on. She switched into hyper-mother-of-cyberbullied-gay-son gear and immediately copied every single message/note/post/website into a forensics file on our computer. I'd already "flagged as inappropriate" several of the videos and photo stills. She fired off a rash of emails to the YouTube, Flickr, Twitter, Facebook, Blogger, GossipRock managers.

But there's no stopping what's released once you open the Pandora's Box that is the internet.

Taking the videos, photos, and messages down was really at the discretion of the social networking sites. Only the most hateful would probably be omitted, but the videos themselves weren't a hate offence.

Essentially, no crime had been committed. No one threatened me explicitly. There was nothing the police could do at this point. Believe me, my mom checked. She called Kato at home, too, but as principal he couldn't do anything, he told her, because the flashmob incident was not a school-sanctioned activity. She wanted to fire off letters to the superintendent and school board, but when we talked it over, she agreed to wait and see what the week at school would bring.

Around eleven pm that night I changed my Facebook profile to private except to friends, and my status to read: *It was only a dance, people.*

My mom and I were exhausted. She went to bed, but I couldn't sleep. And then the phone rang.

"Hello, Jess."

"Ian. Have you seen?"

I sighed. "Yes."

"This is what happens when you're out, Ian."

"What the hell are you talking about?"

"When you come out."

"For shit sake, Jess, this has nothing to do with being out. The whole school pretty much knew or suspected my orientation already. This is about being mean and small. It was a dance. A grad fundraiser. And it got all perverted."

"It is perverted. Being gay."

"No it's not, Jess."

"For me it is."

"I'm sorry you feel that way. But I don't. I'm not sorry for being gay. I'm not sorry for being out. And I'm not sorry for how I feel about you."

"I told you not to make it obvious, Ian. I told you." His voice sounded stricken.

"Jess! I was caught up in the dance. The words of a song. No one knows about us!"

"Well they could, Ian. They sure as shit know how *you* feel. My dad could find out about us."

"Does he use the computer?"

"Only to answer his own email. He doesn't know much else to do with it."

"Then you're safe."

"Someone could send him something. A link."

"Oh, for god sake. How likely is that?"

"Doesn't matter, Ian. It's over."

"What are you saying, Jess?"

"We're done."

And the phone went dead in my hand.

Stupified. Stunned. Stupid. That's how I felt. I'd let him back in and Jess Campeau had stormed around in my heart and my life and then stormed out again.

I wanted to call Tilly. I wanted to wake up Mom. But instead I just sat in the dark and relived it all. The kiss in the change room. Our first meeting. Subsequent clandestine dates. My spring dance performance and the fateful night of his dad's attack. Weeks of abandonment and grief. Our tentative reconciliation. Ending with the Saturday high of the flashmob and the crash and burn of this night.

Some people say that guys don't and shouldn't cry. That it's not masculine. Manly. I don't buy that. Maybe if more boys and men cried, the world would be a healthier, saner place. I don't know, but I think so. My mom always says that she feels a great weight off her shoulders after the occasional good sob-fest. I get that tears are kind of an important release. Why should it be different for guys? Whether straight or gay guys? It's that femme-y idea again. Guys who cry are like guys who dance. Prancing nancies. But I'm not effeminate, despite the male dancer stereotype. And I do cry and I did cry much of that night.

Not just for myself and all the loss and betrayal I was feeling, but also for Jess. I suspected that his dad already knew his son was gay. That the beatings and threats were some form of defence mechanism against the inevitable. The son will come out. If not tomorrow. Someday.

At least I hope so. Because the alternative for Jess could be absolutely deadly.

Living with a lie cost my Great-uncle Léon his life.

Myself, I can't live a lie. I am what I am. Or so the famous Broadway song goes. And I believe those words.

I also believe I can find a place—just like Jess can, if he wants to—where I'll be accepted.

It won't ever be the closet.

After about two hours of sleep, I rose and put the tea bags my mother gave me for the swelling—tactfully withholding all comments—on my eyes for fifteen minutes. That helped a little. So did the long hug she gave me before I went out the door.

Erika was waiting for me at the corner. Tilly joined us when we passed hers. The other three Solid Gold Hip Hop Hotties met us in front of the school. We entered the hallowed portal. Together.

We got a lot of stares, for starters. A few sneers from some of the likely suspects. A wad of spit narrowly missed me. Mercifully, the bell rang. We split off to our separate classes. I made it safely to physics. Jess chose not to attend that morning.

Throughout the day, I kept a low profile. After all, I know about being invisible. In this instance, it served me well. And the day crawled by.

After my last class of the day, Mr. Monaghan found me in the hall and asked to speak to me privately in the Social classroom.

"How are you doing, Ian?"

"Ok, under the circumstances."

"I saw some of the YouTube clips and blogs. The culprits are just smart enough not to cross the line and have their crap taken down."

I nodded.

"This kind of behaviour has gone on since time immemorial," he sighed.

I guess he'd know. World history is Mr. Monaghan's speciality. "Yeah. I figure I'm lucky. In Hitler's era I would have been forced to wear a pink triangle and fared much worse."

"True. But here we are in the twenty-first century, in a developed nation, in a pseudo-urban centre, living a too-familiar story. Don't let this be a defining moment in your life, Ian. Don't let them embitter you. Don't let the bastards win."

"I won't Mr. M."

"You can come talk to me, whenever, okay Ian?"

"Thanks."

"There are many ways to be a man, Ian. And the way you're handling this? You're already more of a man than any of the Neanderthals who are harassing you."

Mr. Monaghan's words buoyed me up. I squared my shoulders and headed for my locker. Somebody had kicked the door repeatedly. It had a bunch of dents and was hard to open. I pretended not to care. Grabbed my coat and books, slammed the door shut. Clicked the lock and turned to leave.

Brittany Westlock stood before me, smacking her gum. A few of her bubble-headed friends, all hair and nails and fake tans, posed nearby.

I tried to walk around her, but she barred my way.

"You got a thing for Jess?"

I heaved a sigh and waited.

"He's taken." There was an ugly edge to her voice.

"I know that, Brittany."

"And he's not interested, if you know what I mean."

"I know exactly what you mean."

"I got nothing against you being gay. Some of my best friends are gay."

As if, I thought to myself but said nothing.

"He's mine."

I could have answered a thousand ways: 'As far as you know,' 'that's what you think,' 'he's just not that into you,' 'only if you have a sex change, and even then it'd be unlikely,' 'Jess is definitely *not* a tit man,' 'not in this lifetime.' But all I said was, "Got it."

She let me pass, her girlfriends tittering at my back. I left the school and ran to the studio.

I was working at the barre in one of the smaller studios when Madame came in.

"Ee-an."

I continued to work on my attitude.

"Your mother telephoned me. To tell of ugliness. Is cruel, the world, sometime."

I moved to arabesque.

"Is not fair. This place sometimes is so beckward." She paused. "I loved a boy."

I held my pose. And my breath. A confidence from Madame Isadora Branislov?

"Once. He was famous dancer. Brilliant. I was young, naïve ballerina. In France."

I released and moved into first position. Began a series of pliés and relevés.

"It was not to be. Rudik and me. He not loving women. Not in that way. My heart break. I watch him soar. Away. From me. To spotlight. To other loves.

"I'm saying only this. I warn you of love. Before. I think of you and dance only. Future. Your great career. But is not wrong to love. Love is never wrong. Whomever we may to love. I want you to know. What I think."

Madame turned to go and in her movement I realized her age. She always seems so ageless, but for a moment, I saw otherwise.

"What happened to the dancer, Madame? Where is he now?"

"He dies," her voice was barely above a whisper. "Many years ago. From AIDS."

"I'm sorry, Madame."

She turned back to me. "Oh, Ee-an. I am also. For heem. For you. But not for having to know love."

Madame observed my développé. Raised my chin slightly with her hand.

"You are strong boy, Ee-an. This too will pass."

TWENTY-TWO
Cuts Like a Knife

The week slogged on. Jess returned to school. He ignored me. I ignored him. It was all how he wanted things to be. And it hurt like hell.

I kept to myself. The Hotties insisted on eating lunch with me. Erika or Tilly or both walked me home. Truthfully, my posse of girls had my back. I even had nicknames for them: Tilly the Titan, Storm-Troopin' Stacey, Death-Force Erika, Terminator Trish, Maelstrom Melanie. I'm sure gums were flapping about the gay boy needing girls to protect him. I didn't need protection. I needed allies. Girls, especially these ones, were strong and beautiful allied forces. I wish more people could recognize how powerful XX can be.

On Friday, the finished "official" version of the flashmob video was up on the school website and on YouTube. It blew all the amateur clips out of the water. And diverted people's attention, to a certain extent. Despite what had happened, despite Jess's rejection of me, I was proud of us—the dancers, the filmmakers. Even Erika and her Goth-girl vision. We'd done a wicked job.

Rogers was over the top about the video. They handed the Whitleigh Graduation Committee a cheque for a nice chunk of change. Cathy Simco was delirious, all her grad prez financial worries solved.

I dared to hope that the other video clips would be lost and forgotten in the internet jungle.

Erika was pretty satisfied with herself, too. But I couldn't blame her. She'd been decent to me throughout the whole flashmob scenario, from beginning to end, and this week, in the aftermath, she'd been solid as a rock. I remembered our shaky start and shook my head at the transformation between us. Dared to think that my danse macabre mate was becoming a friend.

So why was I surprised when Erika approached me that same day with her next ruse?

"I'm starting the Whitleigh GLBTQQ Club."

"Jesus, Mary and Joseph!"

"They're welcome, too!" She grinned her pointy-toothed grin. "Whitleigh's official Gay Lesbian Bi- Transexual Queer and Questioning Club."

"I know what it means. Do you care nothing for your life, Erika?"

"What? You just want to hunker down for the rest of yours, Trudeau?"

"No. That's not what I want."

"Good then. Besides, do you think you're the only one who has ever been a target? I'm a Goth. And emo-chick. I've been called my share of unflattering names. Pushed around by intolerant ass turds. Hate-texted. We misfits have to stick together."

Her determination made me feel drained of blood.

"I'm not sure I'm up for your new club, Erika."

"Why the hell not? You're not the only one, you know, Ian. There have to be other kids, feeling mixed up and scared, slinking around these halls. This isn't just about you."

"Of course not."

"You could do some real good. *We* could, with this club."

"I'm just not that interested in you know… opening myself up to further ridicule, especially right now, or being president of…"

"Who said *you* were going to be president?"

So Erika became chair of Whitleigh's Straight-Gay Alliance club. Mr. Monaghan, who agreed to be our teacher supervisor, convinced her to change the name of the group to invite dialogue and promote trust between students. He also convinced her to be chair rather than president, so as to avoid, in his words, "any hierarchical power structures or struggles," and he convinced Kato of the necessity for the group. How he did this is anyone's guess. Mr. Monaghan has a kind of magic about him.

Our first meeting was a Thursday after school. Predictably, it was Tilly, Stacey, Trish, Melanie, Erika, Mr. M., and me. I was worried some of the school cyber-cretins would crash the club, but when I thought about it, I realized that no homophobic straight person—or GGPS (Gay Guy Playing Straight) as Tilly now refers to Jess—would be caught dead attending. After all, people might talk. Rumours would fly. Reputations would be risked. Lives would be lost. It was a matter of black and white. Don't attend equals straight and narrow and safe. Attend equals flaming queer faggot scumbag.

Although I was initially hesitant about the group, it was a pretty good inaugural session. Still conscious of Erika's previous biting criticism, I shut up and listened. Answered questions when asked. Everyone was concerned for me. That felt… well, good.

And then we moved on, beyond me and my little life. That felt good, too. To stop thinking, obsessing about myself, even if only for a few moments.

We worked on a rad mission statement. Tilly did most of the wording, and we helped edit. *Mission Statement for Whitleigh Composite High School's Straight-Gay Alliance: To make Whitleigh a safe and welcoming place for students. To provide opportunities to build acceptance and understanding between people. To respect all persons, regardless of sexual orientation or gender identity.*

Collectively, we felt that our group could align with SPAM, our human rights/environmental club, because of their compatible objectives. Our first joint SPAM-SGA project would be to invite a speaker from the local Pride Chapter to share information and facilitate a discussion. Members from both SPAM and Straight-Gay Alliance would create posters and advertise throughout the school. Each of us would reach out to people in Whitleigh who might be interested in and open to attending. Tilly also believes that all gatherings require food, and so we each signed up to make cookies or cupcakes. Except that Mr. Monaghan signed up to bring chips. Apparently, he started a fire the last time he used his oven.

We agreed to reconvene in a week. Melanie, who is a pretty good artist, offered to design the poster. Tilly said she'd contact the local media. Erika and Trish were to do further promotions, and I was to liaise with our local Pride Chapter.

Not bad for a start.

Afterwards, I went for a workout. Jess was there at the gym with McDade, working on the universal weight machines. His face was a mask when he saw me. McDade said something to him, and they both snorted and laughed. I started my warm-up on the treadmill. By the time I had finished, they were both gone. With a weird mixture of relief and disappointment, I finished my reps and walked home. Feeling very alone.

Eventually, I stopped waiting for the phone. It was hopeless. Ridiculous.

Jess Campeau had washed this boy right out of his hair.

I had to get that through my thick skull.

But whenever I saw Jess, my heart would speed up, stupid in hope. He never gave me any indication that he knew I was alive. Or cared that I lived.

I wondered if I'd ever get over him.

So I busied myself with routine. And the days thudded by like hammers.

TWENTY-THREE
Fear of Love

"**M**y cousin is two-spirited." Tilly's voice was unwavering in the auditorium. "In many First Nations cultures, the two-spirited person is a visionary, a healer, an artist. Even a spiritual guide."

"I've heard that's true," our speaker from Pride, Alex acknowledged. He was a neat-looking guy, probably in his twenties because he said he was in the final year of his university degree in Political Science. He didn't present gay at all. In his understated jeans, casual white shirt and vest, Alex was well…just a guy. But he had admitted that he was gay. In a relationship with someone. And out.

"It's also true that, historically, homosexuality in many cultures was not viewed as unnatural. In fact, our understanding of sexuality has varied from culture to culture and from era to era. I think we need to begin thinking of sexuality as a spectrum. Many believe that there's no one 'natural' sexual orientation, nor an either/or kind of separation between heterosexual and homosexual. We can be attracted to many people in a lifetime, of either or both genders. Many people experiment with sexuality and re-examine their sexual identity. We don't really have a name for every kind of person along the sexuality continuum. So while sometimes labels are helpful, it's good to recognize that sometimes they can be damaging."

Erika spoke up, "I think it's important to see the person first. Not the label. Not even the way the person looks or acts. But to get to know the human being. At least that's how I feel."

"That's a great point," Alex smiled.

I put up my hand. "What do we do for—for the person who is struggling with his sexual identity. A person who feels he can't come out?"

Our speaker considered this carefully. "There's not much you can do, really, is there? Except listen. Try to be a good friend. I mean it's up to the individual. It comes down to individual choice. And if we value that… I mean that's what we say we value in a democratic society, then we have to honour that person's choice. We're all entitled to some measure of privacy—despite the thousands of surveillance cameras turned on us in public spaces everyday—we all have that right to keep our inner selves to ourselves, right?

"I know as someone watching someone who's closeted, it can be very hard. That's happened in my own life; I have friends who simply feel they can't come out. Or they come out and return to the closet. They have their reasons. Who am I to judge? But I sympathize with you, if you're the friend of someone like that. It's hard to witness."

Understatement of the year.

"I wonder why," I heard Tilly's voice again, "people are so afraid of love. Of different kinds of love. I just don't get it. Why aren't we more afraid of racism? Of war? But love? It just doesn't make sense."

"No," Alex agreed quietly. "It doesn't."

He stayed around to answer more questions after his presentation. About thirty people had attended, some teachers, others SPAM members, and a few interested students I'd not seen before. As the people trickled out, I helped Alex put away his computer projector and displays.

"This friend you talked about," he focused on wrapping up the power cord on the AV-cart. "Someone close to you?"

"Kinda."

"Someone you like casually? Or someone you like romantically?"

"I guess I- I- like romantically."

"Well, that must suck."

"Big time."

"He'll probably work his way through it all." He looked at me. "Maybe not before you finish high school."

"Probably not."

"Here, Ian. Take this," Alex handed me a small business card. "If you ever just need to talk."

"Thanks."

He turned to say goodbye to the few of us remaining. Shook Mr. Monaghan's hand, Erika's, and then mine.

"This is a great thing you're doing here at Whitleigh. A courageous thing."

I shook my head and nodded at Erika. "It was all her idea."

"Good on you, Erika."

"The devil made me do it," she nudged me.

I put the day and Alex's card away in a very secure place, for safe-keeping.

And tried to get on with my life.

The smear campaign on the internet was dying a slow death. Thankfully. I had new friends to spend time with. A new club. Dance dreams for my future.

And I felt the loneliest I had ever been.

At the studio, I found some kind of solace in Barber's beautiful *Adagio for Strings* and Glenn Gould's *Goldberg Variations,* especially the achingly lovely *Aria* of his final recording. Ennio Morricone's haunting "Tema d'Amore" from *Cinema Paradiso* became a kind of anthem. The strains were so familiar to me that the music was part of my breathing.

And so I lived and moved my loneliness through my body.

TWENTY-FOUR
I Kissed a Girl and I Liked It

At school, grads-to-be were frothing themselves into a frenzy over the much-anticipated event of our entire lives. Honestly, it was enough to make me nauseous if I hadn't already been so nauseated. Grade twelve girls were overheard planning their great hair expectations. Comparing grad gown costs. Guys were ganging together to rent limos. Graduation is an annual boon for business in our burb. Tanning salons were booked to overflowing. Flower shops were bursting with colour. Hair salons had to schedule extra shifts of stylists to keep up with graduand demand.

And above all, liquor sales were skyrocketing.

Tilly was aglow about her grad date with Howie. I tried to be interested. Assured her that she would be the most beautiful grad there. She waved my compliment away, but I knew she appreciated it. I hadn't been the most attentive friend these past weeks.

So I rallied myself to make up for it.

On the night before our graduation, I went over to Tilly's house. After all, a girl needs her gay boyfriend to help her prep for her grad date.

She was posing à la Cinderella going to the ball in front of her full-length bedroom mirror. The same one we'd karaoked in front of only about a bazillion times. My heart caught in my throat. As the sappy song goes, when exactly did she go from crayons to perfume? My tomboy chum was transformed to princess.

The dress was as stunning as I remembered. On her feet, those same two usually encased in mud-caked soccer shoes, were the lemon pumps.

"Ian," she tripped towards me and caught herself in time before falling on her face. "You have to help me learn to walk in these!"

We laughed and I took her hand. We experimented on many different surfaces: her mother's hardwood, the concrete of the basement, carpet and lino. And we spent a long time going up and down stairs, a virtual stairmaster workout. But Tilly gained her footing and her confidence. The tutorial ended with a few dance steps in heels. Not quite as successful, but certainly passable. I beamed at my student and was beaming still when she appeared at her bedroom door re-clad in her usual jeans and T-shirt.

"I have something to show you…" Tilly pulled me into her room and handed me a little package, just a little smaller than a shoebox.

"For me?"

"No, loser. This is for you!" Tilly indicated the gift bag, stuffed with gold sparkly paper, sitting on her desk. "But open this first."

I lifted the lid and unfolded the tissue paper within to reveal the little yellow clutch purse. The one we couldn't quite afford from the store with the odious shop clerk.

"Tilly! Did you get a job?"

"Nope, just a gift certificate."

"Uh huh."

"Seriously." She took the delicate handbag and slipped it over her wrist. "I wrote a letter. To the regional manager of La Fabrique. And sent a copy to the head office in Montreal."

"What did you say?"

She gave me her broadest Tillster grin. "Oh, a lot of things. I wrote from the perspective of a Métis woman. Talked about racism, racial profiling. How I thought the store might want to consider sensitivity training for its staff. That sort of thing. All very polite. And in both official languages." She opened and closed the little gold clasp of the clutch. "In return, they sent me a lovely letter of apology *and* a gift certificate. I took that sucker to the store the next day. By myself. It took two and a half hours return trip by bus. Worth every moment. And I got this here little baggie."

"Tilly Monpetit!"

"That's me."

"You are a hunka hunka burnin' love!"

"No doubt!"

Speechless with pride, I handed Tilly her grad gift. She unwrapped it with typical Tilly gusto. A silver bracelet crafted by a local Native artist. I'd had her name inscribed on the inside.

"It's beautiful, Ian!"

She gave me a black satchel with an adjustable padded shoulder strap. "It's for carrying your stuff around at the National Ballet School."

We hugged each other. Though it had once seemed far away, the dance school and the time of our separation loomed close ahead. I would miss my wonderful, brave friend.

It was getting late and I made motions to go.

"Ian. Promise you won't wimp out on me at grad. Promise that you'll still come to the banquet and dance tomorrow."

Thus far I had only consented to attend the pomp-and-circumstance afternoon graduation ceremony, although I had purchased tickets for the evening festivities. Back in January when it all seemed like so much fun. "Don't feel much like dancing, Tilly."

"Ha ha. Funny."

"I mean it."

"That's about all you've been doing lately."

"Not that kind of dancing."

"Not even with me?"

"You'll be with Howie."

"Only some of the time. And Howie can't dance to save his life."
I sighed.

"He isn't worth it, Ian."

"Who isn't?"

"Don't play dumb. You know who. That jackass jockstrap shouldn't ruin your time. Your grad. Just ignore him. Besides you'll be with Howie and me."

"Three's a crowd, Tilly."

"Three's a ménage à trois, Ian."

We laughed. She jumped on me, tackling me so that we tumbled to the floor, then pinning me with those strong soccer girl legs of hers.

"Promise me you'll come! Promise or… or I'll kiss you with my tongue!"

"Eeww! Hetero girl kisses!"

"Yup! You'll kiss a girl and you'll like it. One smooch from these lips and you'll be a straight guy. And your boyfriend won't mind it."

"Ha ha. Boyfriend. As if."

"I mean it. Unless you promise you'll come!!"

"Fine. Yes. Okay." Gasping and laughing.

"Promise?"

"I promise! Alright. Promise."

And then very sweetly and softly, she kissed me on the lips. And I kissed her back.

I love Tilly.

I'd like to say that I had the graduation like those you read about. The kind that get made into Hollywood movies. You know the happy kind. Not the kind like Stephen King's *Carrie*.

I wish I could say that Jess got over himself. That he came over to me at the banquet. Actually asked me to dance. In front of the entire school population. Then took over as my official grad date. Took me home. Just like in a made-for-TV movie.

But none of that happened.

This is what did.

TWENTY-FIVE
Boom Boom Pow

Grad day arrived sunny and full of false May hope.

My mom took Tilly and me for breakfast. Then she dropped Tilly off at her hair appointment and we went over to Gramma and Grampa's for about a thousand pictures of me in the new suit. I put on my grad gown and cap and there were a thousand more photos. Standing up. Sitting down. With Mom. My hand on her shoulder. My cheeks hurt from all that ape-grinning.

Then as we were getting ready to leave for the ceremony, the doorbell rang. My heart leaped, but, of course, Jess had no idea I was at my grandparents or even where they lived.

So I tried to put on my best I'm-so-flipping-happy-I'm-a-graduand face and opened the door.

"Ee-an!"

"Madame!"

"You look so handsome, my prize." She brushed past me and into my grandparents' living room where she twirled about in her swing cape à la typical Madame entrance fashion. "Good day!" she pronounced to my family.

My grandparents are always taken aback by Madame. Perhaps it was the once-over she was currently giving their decorating tastes. She is such a Euro snob.

"But you must to be so proud of heem."

Everyone spoke at once, tripping over their exuberance for my great achievement of surviving high school.

"Ee-an." I heard a pronouncement coming.

"Yes, Madame."

"Madame has gift for you—now that you are man. You must have man gift."

Mom eyed Madame nervously. She knew all too well about Madame's little tastes. Probably worried that Madame had purchased me a silver flask filled with 100-proof Russian vodka.

But no. Instead she took from within her cape a small box wrapped in silver and black paper.

"Madame," my mom protested, "this isn't necessary."

"But, of course. Ee-an is very special to me. Open, my prize."

I know my mother was shooting me those looks—the ones that are meant as cautionary against accepting gifts from Russian dance instructors who are drunks, even if brilliant. I chose this auspicious occasion to ignore my mother entirely, and ripped into the paper.

It contained a silver foil box that fit in the palm of my hand. And in that box, another velvet box like the kind that hold rings.

I briefly wondered if Madame—fifty years my senior—was proposing to me.

But that was just sick.

So I opened the black velvet box. And inside on the red satin cushion, a tie pin. It sparkled. I could barely breathe. A diamond.

"Oh, Madame!"

"It was my father's from old country. I thought once to give to... but no. Is for you. For keeping safe. For remembering Madame. For being gooood boy." She pinned it to my red silk tie. We looked into the mirror together, she over my shoulder. The pin winked in the light. It matched my earring.

"You have been such sad boy of late, Ee-an. Madame hopes sadness in your heart will soon pass. Sadness will pass, my prize. Will pass. Trust to Madame, pleese. You will become great man, Ee-an. Great dancer! And so someone who is hurting your heart will someday to be sorry. Madame knows."

I was tearing up. And then Madame was. And then she was squashing me to her bosom. Then blowing her ample nose in a kerchief near my ear. And through it all—thank god—my grandparents and mother, especially, held their tongues.

"It's a lovely and generous gift," Mom finally spoke. "A very generous gift." I saw her left eyebrow arch. I picked up my cue.

"Yes, thank you so much, Madame. I will always treasure it."

"And so now to watch magnificent ceremony, da?"

"Yes. Oh, yes." And with much commotion we found the camera, film, sweaters, gum, mints, Kleenex. And finally got out the door only ten minutes behind schedule.

We arrived at the auditorium to find a nervous Tilly pacing out front—her grad gown flapping in the May breeze. She greeted us with much relief and then Grampa had the whole camera thing going again, until Tilly pulled me away from my family and Madame. They wandered towards their auditorium seats while we two scooted along to find our spots in line down the hallway. We were to be arranged alphabetically and, of course, near the front of the line was Jess Campeau. He hadn't seen me, so Tilly just squeezed my arm and urged me onward. I left her at the Ms and took my place in the Ts between Rick Thoroughgood and Dylan Tweedsmuir. They barely looked at me.

Then began the grad marching music and the walk into the auditorium and the endless faces of beaming parents, a trillion camera flashes and cheering, weeping, applauding overdressed families.

Followed by the two most boring hours of my entire life. Which I will never get back.

Some football star from the city bleated on about the virtues of the big game and playing for the team and school spirit and believing you can win win win. Every sports' metaphor and cliché he could possibly cram into twenty minutes. I felt like retching by the end.

Then Kato's fat jowls shaking at how awesome we all were, how awesome we looked, how awesome all our parents were, how awesome the banquet and awesome aftergrad were going to be.

Finished off by a prayer from the minister who never gave a single thought to the one Hindu and one Sikh or my Métis best friend in the graduating class.

And finally the interminable reading out of every one of our two hundred and eighty-nine names. The crossing of the stage. The shaking of Kato's fat paw. The moving of the ridiculous tassel from one side of the grad mortar board to the other.

The rush of gratitude that no one yelled out, "Hey, dance for us Trudeau, ya faggot!" Or some such thing.

And then the saccharine recessional music. "Forever Young." And on Rod Stewart's heels, the requisite Green Day song, the one that hopes you have the time of your life. Then a flurry of grad caps flung into the air.

And it was over.

Thank god.

Tilly and I posed for more photos with both our families. Inside. Outside. Upside-down. Her dad worked up a sweat in his too-tight suit. My grampa couldn't stop beaming, my gramma dabbing at her eyes, Madame fixing my hair, my mom fussing.

Howie sauntered over and Tilly introduced him. We promised to meet for the banquet no later than six pm. She tore off home to get into her evening dress.

I handed my grad gown in at the coat check, pretty much the last grad to do so. Then turned around to discover Jess.

"Hey, Ian."

I couldn't believe that he spoke to me. "Hey."

"That was sure long."

"And boring."

He grinned. "I knew you thought so, too." He looked me over. I felt nervous, but at least I was dressed to the nines. "You look real good in that suit. Nice tie pin."

"Thanks. It's a gift from Madame. You look great, too."

We just looked at each other. I tried not to remember. Anything. Despite the din in the room around us, I felt as if I were underwater.

"Well, gotta go," I lied. I knew if I didn't, my heart might pop out of my chest like that freakish alien thing in the *Alien* movie.

"See you tonight."

"Yeah." I really wished then that I could somehow, somehow beg off. Plead sick. Hell, really get sick. But… I'd promised Tilly.

The banquet itself was everything I'd dreamed it wouldn't be. And less.

Starting off with the grand entrance of the football heroes, already half drunk for the dry banquet. Jess and big-bazoobied Brittany, the glam grad, among them.

He looked like a million bucks.

I felt like a hollow tin can.

You know the kind you kick down the street.

All four couples sat together. And made a lot of noise. Toasting and braying.

"She's a skank. He's a dick. They're made for each other." Tilly gave me a quick hug and turned back to Howie.

I lifted my butter knife. It had something stuck on it from a previous meal. Our waiter thoughtfully brought me clean cutlery. I raised my salad fork in resignation.

Dinner was the requisite limp iceberg lettuce tossed with Kraft Italian dressing. Cold chicken drizzled with something congealed and vaguely gravy-like. Carrots underdone next to some potato mush. But what do you expect in arena seating for 800-plus people?

In fact, all the seating had been arranged by the careful grad banquet committee members who ensured their own places were only with the popular and beautiful. We'd been placed with two other couples, also appropriately losers and outcasts. Ivan Bodnaruk, ace mathematician, and his full-figured date, Debbie. Bruno daCosta, from food studies and his cousin, Angelina. I was the only single, but they did their level best to include me in the droll conversation.

"Where ya off to, next year, Ian?"

"Toronto, hopefully, Ivan."

"Ian's auditioning for the National Ballet School. And he's going to get in the post-secondary program, too! I've got money on it." Tilly had to raise her voice above the stadium ruckus.

"I'm gonna work at my uncle's restaurant and go to chef's school."

"That should be good." I looked across at Bruno who was sweating and wiping his brow with his napkin.

"Yeah. I guess it's in my genes."

"Like dance is for Ian," Tilly chirruped.

"Or soccer for you."

"Math for me," Ivan inadvertently spat out a bit of carrot as he addressed us. I looked away discreetly. Then looked back at our group.

All dolled up and deodorized, they weren't half bad, I concluded. At least they were nicer than certain folks a few obnoxious tables over.

Howie blew his nose into his napkin. Tilly looked at him in horror and then over at me. I smiled in sympathy.

And wondered where we'd all be in ten years. I hoped Tilly wouldn't drag me to the reunion. This was depressing enough.

And then the speeches began. Some were okay. Anthony Chiu, the valedictorian, was pretty good. I went to the can during Kato's. But Mr. Monaghan, my social teacher, said some great stuff about living the good life and the examined life. Our grad committee next took credit for the flashmob idea and video, which they screened for the audience, to thunderous applause. No smartass wisecracks about me. That was a relief. And at least Cathy Simco had the grace to thank Erika.

Our graduating class PowerPoint slideshow was pretty hilarious. The Halloween dance with high school female hotties dressed like devils in clingy red body suits with tails. The Terry Fox run. Christmas concert. Various Whitleigh staff looking tired or hung over or mugging for the camera or just ridiculous or all of the above. Ski trip drunks. Valentine's dance. Some of the school clubs, our SPAM group included.

Individuals who were cool and sought after. Some smart kids winning honours. All manner of jocks, jocks, jocks.

Then Tilly, caught in a tournament-winning soccer goal. Looking like the powerhouse she is.

There was even a shot of me leaping across the dance floor. It was a dramatic photo op. I wondered who took the picture. I heard a smattering of applause and I felt my ears turn pink. Tried not to crane my neck to see if Jess, three tables over, had any special reaction.

Of course, there were eight thousand pictures of Jess. All equally flattering.

Fade to black.

Dessert was tolerable. Chocolate mousse with a chocolate-dipped strawberry. I let Tilly have mine.

Then the dance began. I just sat there while Tilly and Howie cut the rug on the dance floor. An hour passed. Glaciers melt more quickly.

I watched Jess dancing with Brittany. She had two left feet. At least I was granted that much.

Tilly took me for a spin for a fast number, a swing tune. It was pretty fun. We kind of stole the show for a few moments. Everyone around us clapped afterwards. Even Jess Campeau and his stunned bimbette date with her sparkling talons for fingernails.

Finally, I felt I could go home. I'd spent the better part of the evening with Tilly and old Howie. I could leave quietly and head over to the dance studio.

I kissed Tilly on the cheek and shook Howie's hand. I'm sure she was fairly relieved to be rid of me. She could concentrate on just her date. Let her gay friend get along elsewhere to feel sorry for himself.

On my way to the door, I met Erika, who admittedly looked pretty striking in her Morticia Addams formal Goth gown.

"Leaving so soon?"

"Yeah. I gotta go."

"It's your grad night, too, Ian."

"Well, I've graduated."

"Congratulations. You made it." Erika shook my hand.

"You, too. Congrats." I hesitated. "It's been good to—to get to know you, Erika."

"Yeah. Backatcha, Trudeau. You wanker."

Grinning, I turned away, promising myself to google that British expletive when I got home.

I waited for my cab outside. Ignored the huzzahs and burping from the small clot of guys guzzling beer next to someone's van in the parking lot.

I looked up and loosened my tie. It was a starry night, even against the streetlights of our banal burb. The North Star flickered as white as the diamond in my tie pin. How perfect if Jess were here.

And then, quite suddenly, he was.

Pulling me by the arm away from the glare of the streetlights. The car headlights. Around the corner of the auditorium. Into the shadows. Alone. Where we began. The two of us. I heard my taxi drive up. Honk two or three times. Screech away.

And then I heard, "Hey, Campeau. Need any help with the fagboy?"

Jess lurched away.

Unrehearsed, it begins. Our group number.

A tour de force.

From the shadows sounds a bass note hammering a heartbeat. Three figures dart into the shadows. Pull apart the pas de deux danseurs. Hoist the principal dancer onto their shoulders in one swift balletic move. A harsh motif begins—strings and timpanis.

The horizon swims when the three toss the principal, end over end en l'air, into a somersault. He lands just inside the spotlight cast by the streetlamp. Lightning flash, the trio catapult towards the light and him. He is folded à terre as the first, in grand jeté, leaps upon him. In quick succession the principal is visited with a series of frappés, against the thigh, the back, the stomach the head. Lights dance about the danseur's eyes. Music—horns and cymbals—moves to presto.

The principal struggles to rise, and somehow Lazarus stands amidst the ensemble, aware that his partner hovers at the edge of the circle. In a perfect port de bras, he reaches to his partner, but the company surrounds him. In slow motion they propel him around from man to man. He spies a gap. An escape. Seizes the moment.

And bursts free.

Travels across the asphalt. Towards the brighter stage centre lights. His thighs afire. A burning in his shoulder. Stomach whirling. Sweat, blood, snot running down his face. Mouth swollen to swallow speech. Rising now, the flutes shriek shrill and desperately. Still the dancer dances. Through the pain. Onwards. Away.

But the ensemble in pursuit lunges towards him. True to the choreography of this dance, they take him by the arms, twirl him around in a dark pirouette. The principal's eyes widen. His face a grotesque mask. The trio raises him. He does not struggle, but pulls himself taut. In response, they pull his limbs en croix. And with great force, they throw him down. His body ripples at contact. And the orchestra swells.

A wounded gazelle, the danseur lifts his head, his shoulders. Muscles protest, but the last note has yet to ring.

I looked up into Jess's face, floating above mine. Knew he was going to intervene. Finally. Save me. From these attackers. These brutes.

"I love you," I managed through blood and cracked teeth. And Jess Campeau just walked away.

TWENTY-SIX
Hallelujah

He tried to reach me afterwards.

After the beating.

After the night in Emergency. The twenty-seven stitches. Resetting of my nose and jaw. The frozen gel packs for the swelling and Demerol for the pain. The visits to the dentist. The assault charges pressed against the guys. After my conversation with the RCMP a few days later where I named names through my wired mouth. Even spelled them out. M-C-D-A-D-E. G-R-E-E-N-E.

I could have named Jess Campeau. Though he didn't lift a finger. *Because* he didn't lift a finger.

That is, until he tried emailing. Texting. Phoning.

Too little, too late.

After the news splash in the *Herald Weekly:* "Grad Bashing Sobers Whitleigh High School." After a penitent Mr. Kato tried to pay me a visit but Mom barred him at the door.

Jess tried to reach me.

After I wept. Not like a girl. A beaten young man.

Beaten.

It could have been worse. They could have come at me with baseball bats. Taken out my kneecaps so that I could never dance again.

But it was bad enough. A bad enough beating that it was immediately clear to the ambulance attendants, the doctors, my mother, and me that National Ballet School is out for this year.

He called. Repeatedly. Left messages. I never took the calls or returned them. Despite the threat of his father finding out, Jess bombarded me with emails. I deleted every one. He dared to use his cellphone to contact me. My text message inbox was full.

Ian, call me.

Ian, I'm sorry.

Ian, FTLOG. Call. I'm up. It's midnight.

I'm sorry.

Call me.

I'm sorry.

Call me.

I'm sorry.

I'm sor…

I erased every message. My inbox filled again. I erased those, too. Deleted him from my Facebook friends.

Everyone who is my *friend* knows where to talk to me in person and how to find me.

Apparently, Erika first found me, unconscious. Who knows what brought her outside that starry night? She's the one who dialed 911. Stayed with my mangled self until the ambulance came.

I heard that the whole flashing lights and bloody mess thing put quite the damper on the grad celebrations. Not enough to kill the aftergrad party, but apparently, it was a pretty subdued affair.

Tilly didn't go. Neither did my Goth girl saviour. They both visited me in the hospital, instead.

But I don't remember much after the beating. I was pretty much out of it the first night and the next day. After the repairs to my jaw, once the doctors figured I was out of any potential danger, they let me come home. But I was sure banged up and incapacitated. For the first while there was a ringing in my ears that wouldn't go away. Along with a wrenching in my heart. But both are gone now.

Mostly I slept. And watched a ton of TV. *So You Think You Can Dance. Dancing With the Stars.* And my mom wore herself out renting DVDs. Old classics like *Let's Dance, Daddy Long Legs, Singing in the Rain.* Stuff from the 1970s and '80s like *The Turning Point, All That Jazz, White Nights,* and *Dirty Dancing.* The always wonderful *A Chorus Line* and the doc about its history, *Every Little Step.* And my all-time fave, *Billy Elliot.* My mom found some ballets at the public library, too. Nureyev and Fonteyn in *Les Sylphides.* Baryshnikov in *Don Quixote.*

I ate my meals through a straw. Applied for scholarships. Began to recover. At least outwardly. I am still slowly recovering.

Being beaten up makes you think. Gives you time while you heal. Too much time. Or just enough. Depends on your point of view.

While you lick your wounds, inner and outer, while your bruises and contusions turn various shades, while the aches in your body and your heart begin to mend, you begin to think about cowards. Who they are. Why they are.

You begin to think about people who want to kill you just because of the person you love. Or the someone you're attracted to. You begin to realize those people are invertebrates. Afraid of you. More to the point: afraid of themselves.

Afraid of anything different. Anything sensitive. Funny thing about sensitivity. When you think about it, all of the world's great art—music, painting, sculpture, dance, theatre—exists because of it. Sensitivity is also somehow about caring. Caring about others. Caring about the planet. And yet the world is so scared of males being sensitive. Caring. Somehow caring plus sensitive equals girly equals freak equals weak. In case that's all somehow a part of men, too. Because what would that be saying? How would it question what it means to be a guy? What would it say about guydom? About so-called macho men?

While you're lying on the couch in pain and staring at the ceiling and trying to forget a certain someone, you also begin to think about the people who watch and do nothing. Say nothing. Let it go on and on. Without intervening or objecting. Teachers. Principals. Otherwise law-abiding citizens living comfortably, numbly in affluent suburbia. Parents. Coaches. Average joes leading average, unaware, unexamined lives.

And, of course, one dumb gay jock.

They are responsible. For doing nothing. For not speaking up. And so beatings and bullying and cyberbullying continue: against the different or the simple or the vulnerable. Fag thrashings happen everyday, somewhere. Not to mention other hate crimes and violence against the misfit, or misshapen, or the darker-skinned, or the plain unlucky. Victims of intolerance and ignorance.

Well, Ian Trudeau may have been victimized. But I refuse to be a victim. I may have been beaten. But I'm not.

My mom's been helping. Tilly, too. And I've been seeing a psychologist. A family friend. It helps to talk. Even if it hurts.

And it hurts. More than I can put into words.

I found Alex's business card and called him a few times. He's been a good listener, like I aspire to be someday. He says maybe I can come out later this fall to the local Pride chapter. Maybe even tell my story. Someday mentor youth. When I'm finished with the repairs.

Whenever that is.

TWENTY-SEVEN
It Gets Better

It's been four and a half months since grad. I managed to keep my marks up and write my finals. The school arranged for the exams to be proctored at our house. Some district office guy came along to ensure that I didn't cheat. As if. I got my grades mailed to me in August—straight As. And I received a Rutherford Scholarship.

Mr. Monaghan dropped by in June to see me. He was pretty choked up when he did. I'm really grateful to him for visiting. Says a lot about the guy. Why he's my favourite teacher and all. He told me I was a great young man. That I deserved better. One day, I'd get to live the good life. He brought me a card signed by all the SPAM and Straight-Gay Alliance club members and a gift copy of Plato's *Dialogues - Apology*. I'm at the part that's the crucial discussion between Socrates and Crito where Socrates insists that the good life is the most valuable and that a good life means being just and honourable. I put the card up on my bedroom wall bulletin board. To remind me that a good life is still possible and that there are good people in the world.

Good people like Erika, who has become my frequent Goth visitor. She lives on my block, after all. E-Gothgirl especially liked when my jaw was wired shut. Called it my Trudeau karma. I could only half-snicker at her remark through my mouth wires. On Canada Day she brought over two flags: a Canadian flag and a rainbow flag. Together, we raised them on either side of our Trudeau front door. They're probably flapping away in the autumn wind right now.

Tilly received a soccer scholarship to attend the local city university. I'm very proud of her, but I'm seeing less of her now that fall term has started up. So far she's having a blast. Post-secondary agrees with her. She seems so grown up in her new varsity hoodie, her first-year science texts weighing down her backpack. I hope we don't drift apart, and I'm struggling with the idea that maybe it's inevitable.

Some days are pretty boring. It's hard to watch your friends go off to their lives when your own is on hold.

And as for those who aren't my friends? Well, I heard that Jess Campeau—who finally stopped calling and texting—has joined the army. Like his father before him. I support our troops and all. I watch the news everyday; I want the men and women who serve overseas to come home. Safely. Not in flag-draped coffins. I wonder if Jess will be headed for Afghanistan after training. I wonder if he'll make it home on his own two feet, or because of an injury, or in one of those coffins. I wonder if he's on some kind of suicide mission. Because of his father. To appease him. And to deny himself. Or to die trying.

I almost called him to ask. Almost. Got as far as dialing his number. But I hung up before it could ring. There's no point. In talking. Or in trying to make him into something I want him to be. That's a cold and broken hallelujah.

Gradually, I've been moving back into my dancing and training routine. With massages and physio. Work at the barre. Stretches. Pas de deux. Nothing too strenuous. I'm grateful to be moving. I'm moving. Moving on.

Nothing in my body was permanently or structurally damaged. The doctor said that my level of fitness—my core strength and muscular development—in many ways spared me from worse injury. I had a concussion and some pretty severe contusions, but the worst of those faded to purplish yellow and then away entirely. After about eight weeks, my jaw was healed. For the first while though, at least facially, I looked like something out of a horror movie. Tilly called me zipperhead until the stitches were removed. The plastic surgeon assures me that the scars will fade to almost unnoticeable. Slowly I'm regaining my boyish good gay looks.

And I'm eating like a racehorse to regain the pounds I lost on my liquid diet. Nothing like Mom's poutine to help with that! I've had enough energy shakes and Ensure for a lifetime. Gag!

As you might expect, Madame practically had a stroke over the whole thing. She's better now, but there was quite the drama when she first laid eyes on me. Imagine something like a cross between a hurricane and a seizure. You get the picture. She brought me a beautiful fruit basket. Tilly made us smoothies with the bananas, all the while uttering every fruity pun she could muster. It hurt to laugh, but what good medicine.

Since then Madame has written a number of letters to the National Ballet School, requesting a deferral and explaining my special circumstances. They wrote back to say that though I was welcome to audition again, they could not hold my place for a year or guarantee that I'd accepted next season. It's all really disappointing, to say the least, but we both feel that if I made it once, I can make it through a second audition for next summer's program.

I hope so. I don't want to miss the chance to dance.

I'm a dancer. Not a victim. And I don't want to live like one.

Though I'll admit I have been sticking fairly close to the cocoon that is my suburban home. My psychologist is working with me to overcome some residual fears I have. About being outside alone after dark. That kind of thing. I'm a little haunted, I guess. Erika has suggested that we go to an after-dark party. Goth girl and gay boy. Can't you just see us?

But I appreciate the gesture. And just maybe I'll take her up on it. I intend to get through this. I don't want to live my life in fear.

I am out. And I'm staying out.

When I check my heart for how I feel about Jess these days, there's not much love there. I guess all the love was pummelled on the battlefield.

But in talking with Alex, my mom, my shrink, I've learned that I haven't given up on love. Maybe for now. But not forever.

That's the kind of guy I am. An annoying, stubborn wanker. Just ask Erika.

A guy determined to break away from this hopeless hamlet and get to Toronto for the four-week, second-stage audition. And hopefully the professional year of training to follow.

No one is going to stop me.

Or force me back into a closet.

Or beat my dreams to pulp.

Not the small citizens of my minor hometown.

Not a pack of homophobic thugs.

Not a spineless gay jock.

Him least of all.

I've been waiting all of my life for this. I am a dancer. Even if I don't make the final cut. I need to show myself and others like me that I can. We can.

I am going to dance to save my life. My heart.

I am going to dance because, like Mr. Monaghan told me and Alex assures me, there *is* more than one way to be a man in this world. More than one way to participate. To make change. For the better. Or at least I'll dance, trying.

And one more final important thing.

I am going to dance Jess Campeau out. Of my heart. My mind. My body.

Every chance I get.

I will. Dance.

Acknowledgements

First off, a huge bow to my mentors, editors and readers of earlier drafts of the novel: Duane Stewart (dear friend and patient editor), Geoff McMaster (my hawk-eyed and constant supporter), Mark Haroun (things go better with Nugan), Carolyn Pogue (we have the same lips), Hilary McMahon (agent extraordinaire), the folks at Great Plains (thanks for picking me)—your gentle guidance helped me rethink and reshape this book. I curtsey in gratitude before Marla Albiston and Eleanor Fazan for their amazing dance expertise and advice, and before Carol McDonald, for hers on all those athletic things I know nothing about. I also wish to salute my dance and movement teachers for their patience and tenacity in trying to make me a dancer. A huge bouquet to my mom, Jeannie Sobat, who taught me at a very young age how to understand and celebrate diversity. Hats off to Glen Huser and Brian Francis for your generosity of spirit. I pop the cork for dear friends, Stephen Heatley (Tiger Baby) and James Tyler Irvine. And I raise a cup to Thomas Trofimuk for being my cheerleader, for not drowning me in the Queen Elizabeth pool, and for my new muse, Sid.

Many gay and straight students—too many to name here— were the inspiration for this story. So here's a Standing O for all of you, and in particular for Michael Munrow, Mark Healy, Ian Sled, Jenn Gould, Rowan Nielson, Kelly Spilchak, Tara

Lathan-Durepos, former SPAM members and leaders, former People of Song members, former Contains Real Juice members, SWYC (Spoken Word Youth Choir), the talented and beautiful youthwriters who've graced the pages of my life, as well as my cousin, Michael Danyluk.

To all the beautiful young people who have come out to me over the years, I salute your incredible courage. I am proud to know you and so grateful that you are in this world. You have much to teach us.

For further information for gay/lesbian/bi/trans/questioning youth:

www.egale.ca

www.gaycanada.com

    (especially the directory at GayCanada Resource
    Directory Youth Services/Jeunesse)

www.youtube.com/user/ItGetsBetterCanada

www.youthline.ca

www.thetrevorproject.org

KidsHelpPhone.ca 1-800-668-6868